Vengeful Spirits

by

Sandy Wolters

Spirit Voices, Book 3

Vengeful Spirits

Cover Art by *The Wild Rose Press, Inc.*

The Wild Rose Press, Inc.
PO Box 708
Adams Basin, NY 14410-0708
Visit us at www.thewildrosepress.com

Publishing History
First Fantasy Rose Edition, 2020
Trade Paperback ISBN 978-1-5092-3274-1
Digital ISBN 978-1-5092-3275-8

Spirit Voices, Book 3
Published in the United States of America

"Hurry! He has a knife. Bright Flower is trying to fight him off."

Time slowed to a snail's pace. His thumping heartbeat dulled all external sound. Nathan didn't think—he didn't weigh his options. Bright Flower was in trouble, and he'd kill any man who would dare put a hand on her. Nathan took the stairs three at a time with Jared close on his heels. He burst through the door and got the fright of his life.

Bright Flower was on her back. A man straddled her body—a knife held above her chest. "Say please! I want to hear you beg for your life."

Nathan propelled himself forward, but Jared caught him. He fought against his friend's hold. "No! Think, Nathan. If you hit him, the momentum could push the knife into Bright Flower. I'll grab his right arm, and you take his left," his friend ordered. "We'll yank him off of her together. It's the safest way."

Bright Flower screamed something in Navajo as her knee slammed into the man's groin. Her forehead connected with the offender's face, and his knife went flying. Having the upper hand, she pushed off with her leg and rolled both of their bodies across the floor. It only took a split second for her to yank a hidden dagger from her boot and press it against the man's throat. "Say, please," she hissed.

Dedication

To my fierce girls, Shandelle, Pilar, Tator Tot,
and my little Great Peanut.
I love you all.

Prologue

Sometimes the ground beneath our feet bears witness to grievous heartache. Tears of the shamed and shunned saturate the land destroying any hope for healing. Malevolence strikes out with every gust of wind. Danger lurks and thrives in every shadow. If you want to live, fleeing is the only option.

A sinister, closely held secret seizes a vast expanse of Northeastern Arizona bordering the Navajo Nation. There is a block of land so cursed, no living soul, human or animal, can survive. Fearful of retribution, the Navajo people—a deeply spiritual community—will not speak of such things.

For years, ranchers have tried to tame the land and failed. Crops will not grow. Livestock mysteriously die shocking and torturous deaths. Over time, the horrific accounts of man and animal alike—being stalked by something terrifying under the cover of darkness have been spread throughout the masses—usually as campfire fodder. To the detriment of anyone venturing onto the property, the superstitious nature of the tales were discounted by the general public as nothing more than vivid imaginings. But the Navajo people know differently and avoid the area at all costs.

To this day tortured screams of the damned fill the night air and mysterious creatures threaten any man drawn to this territory. Vengeance will not be denied.

Chapter One

Nathan's sedan skidded to a stop on the rocky, wash-board dirt road. Glancing at Jursic, he patted his side, making sure the Glock remained tucked securely in its holster. Two dually pickup trucks were haphazardly parked nose-to-nose—blocking the road as if they'd just played a game of chicken. The cabs of both vehicles were empty, their drivers locked in a loud tussle and neither appeared to be aware of the new arrivals. As if the struggle wasn't bad enough, earsplitting, panic-riddled voices saturated the air, amping up the tension to a fevered pitch.

Nathan and Jursic jumped from their vehicle. Uncertain about the parties involved and what circumstance lay behind the struggle, the men were mindful of keeping the heavy-load work trucks as a shield between them and the heated argument. They warily crept toward the unsuspecting brawlers ready to intervene if it became necessary.

A hefty guy, easily Nathan's size at six-foot, five inches tall, did his best to hold onto the shoulders of a much smaller, grizzled old man who seemed to be suffering an attack of hysterics. Wearing heavy suede Sherpa jackets, leather work gloves, worn jeans, cowboy hats, and boots, both men were obviously cowboys. Hell, they even sported old-school six-shooters. There was nothing dime store about these two. They were genuine. Even though Nathan had been born and raised in Arizona, he was urban through and through—a thriving metropolis boy all the way. That being the case he'd never met a *real* cowboy, and up until this moment he'd had serious reservations that any remained in existence.

With surprising agility, the old cowboy wriggled his way free from the larger man's grasp and landed a hard right to the big guy's left cheek. Considering the old geezer's age and size, Nathan was impressed with the amount of force behind the punch. Even so, if a fight ensued, the distraught old man didn't stand a chance. The way Nathan saw this situation playing out was that the old dude was one hit away from a hospital visit or possibly even a casket.

Reassuring himself, Nathan clasped the gun at his side which was still snug in its holster. His fingers itched to pull the weapon free. But for now, they'd stand down and let nature take its course.

Once a cop, always a cop—instincts were ingrained deeply into Nathan's psyche, and during his time on the Phoenix PD he'd learned patience. People never gave straight answers if someone they didn't know started peppering them with questions. But in the heat of anger, they always spilled their guts. Chances were good that they'd know what the problem was between these two before anyone got hurt. But if the big cowboy decided he'd had enough of the old timer's solid blows, he and Jursic would rush in to break up the fight.

With impressive speed, the large man spun the old guy around and trapped him with his arms. Dangling him a foot off the ground, the bigger man grumbled, "Dammit, old man, I told you to cut that out. You need to calm yourself down and talk to me. If you don't, I'm going to have to knock some sense into that ancient, feeble mind of yours."

The quick movement spurred Nathan to pull his weapon. Worried the old guy was about to get some payback, Nathan had finally heard his fill. Grimacing, he glanced at Jursic. "Time to roll, buddy."

Both men leveled their guns and walked into view, startling the big man. It only took a split second for him to release the aged cowboy. Using his massive body as a shield, he shoved the old guy behind him and raised his hands.

Now he's protecting the old codger? Nathan didn't know what to think.

There was steel in the big guy's voice and unfettered rage in his eyes as he hollered, "There's nothing here for you." With his hands still raised, the man stiffened his jaw and took a defiant step forward. "I don't know what you want but scaring an old man out of his wits is pretty damn low if you ask me. You could have hurt him last night." Even with the guns pointed squarely at his chest, the tough cowboy took another gutsy step forward. His eyes darted between Nathan and Jursic, sizing them up. The deep snarl emanating from his throat and fierce sneer spoke volumes. This man was not someone you wanted as an enemy. Even outnumbered, the younger cowboy still searched for ways to beat the odds and get the upper hand.

Impressive. Nathan had to give the man credit. If he'd had less life experiences dealing with hard asses, he might've been persuaded to take a step back. Instead, he and Jursic stood their ground.

"This is my land. I'm not going to ask you to leave. I'm *telling* you. Get out before I'm forced to hurt you."

Nathan couldn't help himself. The man's remarkable audacity in the face of calamity spawned a wide grin. "You wouldn't by any chance be John MacAllister, would you?"

The rancher's arms slowly came down, but his hands flexed and fisted at his side. "Yes. As I said before, this land is *mine*. I don't appreciate it when people draw their weapons on me."

Nathan and Jursic holstered their sidearms and stepped forward with outstretched hands. "Mr. MacAllister, I'm Nathan Gordon, and this is Pete Jursic. I'm the security expert that you hired from Bastion Enterprises. I believe you've discussed safety issues as well as possible missing men with my partner, Jared Bastion."

Ignoring his outstretched hand, the ranch owner quickly moved to within inches of Nathan. His eyes reflected distrust as they squinted. *More sizing up,* Nathan thought. "Bastion said he'd send someone next Monday. Today is Friday."

Nodding, Nathan smiled to ease the tension. "That's correct, sir. But we were in Flagstaff doing some heavy lifting for a big wedding that's happening on Sunday. We had some spare time, so Jursic and I thought we'd get a head start on your security issues. The information my firm received indicated that you wouldn't be arriving until Monday. We take missing men seriously and felt obligated to start the investigation as early as possible. I intended to give you some answers on whoever's targeting you and your ranch hands before you arrived from Montana."

Nathan shoved his hand out farther. "As I said, I'm Nathan Gordon. And this here is Jursic. He's recently left the FBI and joined forces with us in the private sector." Knowing a lot of people from Montana were suspicious of the FBI—or for that matter, any other government agency—Nathan offered a huge grin. "I hope you don't hold the fact that he was a fed against him. I'm working hard to break all of those ridiculous habits the feds insist their agents follow. Once you get to know him, you'll find he's not too bad of a guy."

Nathan's weak attempt at a jest caused the rancher's face to relax, but only a fraction. The man had powerful features, a big block jaw, and a sharp, piercing gaze. Stress lines etched the edges of his gunmetal gray eyes and reflected thinly veiled tension.

Without removing his well-worn glove, the man accepted Nathan's hand and shook it forcefully. To acknowledge Jursic, he halfheartedly nodded in his direction. "Call me Mac." Releasing Nathan's hand, Mac pivoted and gestured to the old cowboy. "This here is Hank. He's been my ranch foreman over in Montana for years."

The old guy appeared dazed. Before responding, the codger whipped his head around to search the trees behind them. Nathan had to clear his throat to get Hank's attention. Seemingly satisfied, the elder cowboy turned and stuck his hand out. "I'm leaving now. I sure hope you can fix whatever the problem is, but…" The old man nervously glanced back to the tree line again and lowered his voice. "Something tells me that this ain't somethin' that can be fixed."

Still grasping Hank's hand, Nathan peered as far into the timbers as he could. A heated prickling sensation crawled up the back of his neck and produced a shiver. That was never a good sign. Squeezing the gloved hand for reassurance, Nathan stated, "Why don't you tell us what the problem is? We're here to help."

"Nope. I've already told Mac everything. I'm leaving—going back to Montana. There ain't nothin' in the world that could keep me here another minute. I know we've just met and all, but you seem like a trustworthy sort to me. Before I leave, I need you to promise you will not let Mac stay on this land. Now mind what I say, boy. That doesn't mean he talks you into staying with him. It means you pick him up and carry him out if he refuses to go, you hear me? Lookin' at your size—" He glanced over at Jursic. "—the size of both of you, you're the men for the job. If you say so, I'll take you at your word and be comforted by your promise."

Mac swore under his breath and tilted his head down. The top of his cowboy hat gently swayed back and forth illustrating his displeasure with Hank's request.

The old man's gaze pleaded with Nathan. How could he possibly refuse? "You have my word."

"Thank you." Releasing Nathan's hand, Hank took a step toward Mac. "I'm sorry, boss. I didn't mean to let you down. I tried. I did. It's just not safe here. I'll see to the Montana ranch while you're busy with this mess." The plucky old man poked Mac in the chest with his index finger. "You heed my words, boy. What's going on here doesn't have a thing to do with people—*living* people that is. No matter how hard you try, you ain't gonna find any one person responsible. There's something wrong with this *place*, this *land*. I can feel it in these old bones of mine. They've never steered me wrong in the past. That's how I've lived to see seventy. And if you were to ask me, I'd tell ya that whatever it is can't be fixed by no citified security experts." Hank turned back to Nathan and Jursic. "No offense."

Jursic chimed in and offered a kind smile. "None taken."

With a bob of the head, Hank jumped into one of the trucks, backed off the road, and spun out past the men—throwing rocks and dirt in the dually's wake.

Continuing to watch the dust cloud, Mac stated, "Get whatever you need out of your car. I'll drive you up to the ranch in my truck. That vehicle of yours won't make the trip." He pivoted and climbed into the truck leaving both men standing in the middle of the road. Nathan shot another glance at the tree line. Sliding his sunglasses down his nose, he tried to search the shadows for any visible sign of danger but came up blank.

"Well, Mac seems like a fun kind of guy." Jursic nervously chuckled before continuing. "I'm looking forward to you throwing him over your shoulder." Shooting a look at the dually, he added, "And here I thought all those men I worked with in the FBI were badasses. I have a feeling *that* guy belongs in a category all to himself."

Pushing his glasses back in position, Nathan grunted. "I don't expect we'll become life-long friends. He's interesting, though. From what I've seen so far, I don't believe that man would back down under any circumstance. I'd say a powerful rancher like that makes a lot of enemies. We're going to have to do some digging into his past. Maybe that's what's going on here. Someone is trying to ruin him." While that scenario made sense, uneasiness lingered just under the surface. Nathan tried his best to shrug the restless sensation off with a quick roll of the shoulders, but it was useless. "Come on. Let's jump in and get the story straight from the horse's mouth."

****

Bright Flower stood the shovel in the corner of the shed and removed her gloves, throwing them haphazardly on the workbench. She bent over and grabbed her knees—the burn of tight kinks in her lower back stretched and started to ease.

The sixteen sheep she had acquired over the last few years were a source of considerable pride. Spending time with them often proved to be a wonderful way to rejuvenate spirit and body from the rigors of practicing the Navajo medicine healing arts. The back-breaking work of keeping their corral clean also allowed a momentary respite from all thought of the turmoil currently screwing up her life.

Her grandfather's incessant matchmaking was driving her crazy. Navajo men seemed to be coming out of the woodwork vying to be her husband. Every day he'd discuss another possible match. As of yet, she hadn't been able to convince the elder that the Creator had already chosen her mate. More importantly, *she* had already chosen her life's partner. This ongoing discussion—dispute was more accurate—had left a deep, uncomfortable rift growing between them. This morning was no different. She'd never forget his venomous words. *"You are twenty-five years old. It is*

9

time to relinquish these childish imaginings. You must remember your lineage, Granddaughter. You are a powerful Navajo Singer and a born witch. Our people's needs must always come before yours. If you are too selfish to think in those terms, then you are obliged to think of your children and their children's heritage. For the sake of our tribe, it is necessary for the powerful healer's energy that courses through our veins be passed down to the next generation. For that to happen, your husband must be one of us—a Navajo."

A deep frustrated sigh escaped as she leaned against the wall. "How on earth can I make this right?" The reason Spirit Keeper was bound and determined to oppose her on this subject was evident. Through dream quest, the man she'd come to love was a white man who knew nothing of the Navajo Way. The traditional ways were fundamental to the everyday lives of Bright Flower and her grandfather. She didn't understand why the Creator had chosen this path and this man for her, but he had. So, this was one of those times in life that old-fashioned beliefs would not win out. *No way.*

This argument was nothing new. Nathan had been a source of agitation between Bright Flower and her grandfather since she was a small child of five. Even though she'd only just met the man in person, she'd spent plenty of time with him nightly through dream quests. Throughout the years, Bright Flower had explained countless times that the Creator allowed her to travel through dreams and spend quality time with Nathan. Even for one so young, she knew he was the man she would one day marry. The obstacles were bountiful when someone of her stature in the Navajo community was involved in an interracial marriage.

Such a thing was not done. From the first time she catapulted to Nathan's side in her dreams, not a night went by that she didn't meet him through dream quest.

Bright Flower had always been encouraged to relay images from her spiritual night travels to her grandfather. He'd told her time and time again that nighttime journeys provided vital visions, some we'd expect and some we wouldn't. Oftentimes, the messages would be jumbled and hard to decipher, but the answers to life's mysteries were always accessible through the quest.

At first, he was thrilled to hear she'd met her future husband. Until, that is, he realized she was talking about a boy that didn't understand their culture or traditions. From that point forward, he'd dismissed everything she'd relayed to him refusing to accept the notion of Nathan becoming a part of their lives. She'd talked herself blue trying to convince him that this was not a passing fancy. There was a deep spiritual connection fostering this relationship. But he'd written off her appraisal of the meaning behind the quests as inaccurate. Every morning over breakfast, she'd discussed childhood adventures in which she and Nathan participated the previous night. It had become commonplace for her grandfather to ignore her while she spoke of such things. If she felt particularly feisty, she would keep talking, refusing to be brushed off. When the grumpy elder had enough, he would slam his fist on the table and storm out of the room unwilling to listen to another word.

All of these many years later, the Navajo elder continued to reject the man she believed would be her future husband. Even after Nathan popped up in the flesh at a friend's wedding a few months ago, Spirit Keeper refused to listen to reason. The submissive role her grandfather expected—no—demanded—her to play in public did not allow her to approach the man she'd loved for a lifetime.

Our relationship is so different when I'm alone with Grandfather. Spirit Keeper treats me as an equal. My opinions matter to him on all things but Nathan. The elder not only allowed speaking her mind when they were in private but enjoyed the spirited conversations that her insights provoked. But sadly, Navajo tradition would not tolerate such displays in public. If she were to forget her place, the great Spirit Keeper would lose face—and that was strictly prohibited.

If only she'd met Nathan in person that first time in a private setting. She would've reached out to him in a heartbeat. Life would've been vastly different today if she could've just been herself in that brief moment in time.

In the past, out of respect for her grandfather, she'd given in on important issues, but under no circumstance would she budge on the subject of Nathan.

Huffing out a breath, she angrily spat out, "Grandfather is usually so in tune with messages from beyond and has never questioned spiritual communications before. Why is he being so dang difficult about this?" Wiping her brow, Bright Flower tightened her resolve to do what was right. "Well, if Nathan is worth having, he's worth fighting to keep. Grandfather *must* come around to my way of thinking because I will not marry another."

Bright Flower yanked a bucket from beneath the

workbench and turned it upside down to use as a makeshift chair. A mud and dung mixture that smelled to high heaven stuck in clumps to her galoshes. Rattlesnakes and scorpions needed a warm, dry space in the late winter months too, so it was impossible to leave her rubber boots outside. Not wanting to mop the trailer floors again, she put her misery to work, slid off the footwear, and whacked clods of muck from her boots. Needing a shower anyway, she wasn't concerned about the stinky mixture as it flew in all directions.

As her shoes took the brunt of her anger, a tiny black and white kitten bumped against her leg, demanding attention. Momentarily tossing the galoshes aside, she picked the animal up and cradled it in her arms. Kissing the small critter on the nose, she continued her story without fear of being dismissed. "I'm telling you, Mósí yázhí, the first moment I laid eyes on Nathan was electric. Our gazes met briefly, and I could tell he recognized me, but then he looked away. I was so shocked to see the man whom I'd grown up with—the man who had invaded my nights since we were children that I whispered his name. Grandfather overheard and chastised me, but not before he got a good look at the person who had caused so many problems between us."

She nuzzled the small animal and whispered, "Nathan didn't say a word or even look in my direction the rest of the night." Holding the kitten out so she could speak directly to the animal, she stated, "It broke my heart that he walked away from me. Since Grandfather was sitting right next to me, I didn't dare call out to him." She scowled and hissed, "Grandfather seemed beyond pleased over the rebuff. The rejection gave him the ammunition needed to disregard any connection there may have been between Nathan and me.

"Oh Mósí yázhí, I haven't heard a word from the man since that night. But..." she scratched the kitten's chin and smiled, "my dreams have changed for the better. Somehow, we feel more connected. Our nightly meetings are more meaningful.

"Why hasn't he called on me yet? Convincing Grandfather that Nathan is my destined husband would be much easier if the man showed some interest—any interest at all."

A loud honk from a vehicle startled her. She nuzzled the kitten one last time and looked out the shed's door. "We have a visitor, Mósí yázhí. I don't recognize the truck, so someone must be ill. It's time to go to work. I'll bring you some milk later."

Gathering her rubber boots and work-gloves, she hoped that whoever was sick could wait until she showered. Otherwise, it was going to be a long, uncomfortable afternoon.

Just as she shoved the shed door closed, Spirit Keeper rushed out of the trailer and yelled, "Bright Flower, come quickly! You have a guest. His name is Martin."

Chapter Two

Being the newbie, Jursic was assigned the back seat. After five minutes of silence, Nathan turned to face the cowboy driving. "So how big is this ranch?"

"The Arizona branch of the Aces and Eights is right around one hundred thousand acres. To the north, there's a small strip of state land between my property and the Navajo reservation. To the south are the White Mountains and the Apache reservation. The eastern boundary is the Arizona State Route 191."

Silently mulling the information over Nathan couldn't help but squirm in his seat. He would never bring up superstitions with a new client, but everything Mac had said gave him pause. Growing up with Jody, his resident ghost whisperer, and being friends with Rainy, a Wiccan High Priestess, he immediately recognized the red flags. Not believing in coincidences, what he'd just learned left him a little rattled. Mac's ranch, The Aces and Eights, was named after a poker hand—the notorious dead man's hand. If that weren't bad enough, the property bordered the Devil's highway—old Route 666. Back in 1993, Arizonans had been so freaked out by the bizarre occurrences on the highway that the road number had been changed to 191. From some of the legends he'd heard over the years—including the ghost stories his dad enjoyed conjuring around the campfire years ago to scare the crap out of him and his siblings—the name change hadn't done anything to alleviate the strange events that frightened travelers on the ill-fated highway.

Tucking away that nugget of information, he continued his questioning. "When did you take ownership of the land? Do you know any of the previous owner's history?"

"I bought the land about three months ago from an estate. I was told it hadn't been a working ranch in over seventy-five years. There's a rundown house on the property that is usable enough for my needs. Right now, it's in no condition for anyone other than my cowboys. But it's got good bones. I planned for my men to fix it up, but none of them were here long enough. Before sending the hands out here, I spent thousands of dollars bringing electricity to the house. The best I could tell, the home used to run on propane. I've thrown a huge amount of money into this investment, and no one is going to make me back away. Those that would try don't know me."

Nathan raised his eyebrows while he waited for more of an explanation. When none was forthcoming, he pushed on. "Getting back to your men, can you tell me where they went or why they left? If possible, I'd like to talk with them."

Mac clenched his teeth. Deep worry lines etched his brow. "Truth be told, this is my first trip to the property to stay for an extended period of time." Taking his eyes from the road, Mac stared Nathan down. "And before you say anything, yes. I plan on staying here."

Nathan shot the man a cocky grin. "We'll see about that. I'd hate to disappoint Hank. I have a feeling that old man doesn't take too kindly to people breaking their promises. Please continue with what you were saying."

Mac didn't look happy but thankfully didn't pursue the argument. "Before purchasing the land, I flew over every square inch. Because I'm not familiar with this area, my men were sent ahead to plot the ranch's property lines, find water, access roads, and anything else needed to run cattle.

"The first group I sent…" Mac stumbled on his words and sighed as his gaze shifted from the road to look Nathan in the eye. Nathan was willing to bet that a man like Mac kept his feelings at bay. He'd probably be pissed if he realized just how transparent his facial expressions were at the moment. "There were five men. Not my best and most reliable, but good enough for the job at hand. At first, I was getting reports from them every few days. Then nothing. All communication stopped with no explanation. I don't know exactly how long they stayed, but they were here for at least two weeks. Maybe a little longer. After the third week passed and no one had heard from them, I contacted the local Sheriff's office in St. Johns and asked them to do a welfare check. They called me back and said there was no sign of the men and they didn't believe foul play was involved. Based on that information, I wrote them off as walking off the job and sent another three men. When the replacements arrived, they reiterated what the Sheriff's office had told me. It looked to them as if the men had just up and quit without notice. The new group said they'd stay and finish surveying the surroundings. Two weeks later, we lost contact with them.

"This is a tough area. There is no cell service here.

You have to drive almost all the way to St. Johns to use a phone. That's about seventy miles away, mostly on slow going dirt roads. The main dirt road off of Highway 191 is a little wash boarded but good enough to travel on with some speed. But once you turn onto the ranch road, it's a bumpy ride."

As if proving his point, they hit a pothole. The truck lurched to the side bouncing hard enough to jostle the men. "See what I mean? If I were you, I'd put my seatbelt on. It's only going to get worse from here."

The road narrowed significantly. While the vehicle continued down what appeared like nothing more than a game trail, Nathan and Jursic snapped themselves in for safety. Nature had reclaimed this part of the road. Scrub oak and mangled cedar scraped and scratched at the side of the truck.

"For safety, I supplied all of the men with radios so they could communicate with one another. My ranch hands are aware that danger is always part of the game in this type of environment, and they take it seriously. There are a multitude of issues that could arise at any given time. Your horse could come up lame. You could get bit by a rattlesnake. Before you know what hit you, the heat in the summer months can go to your head. Powerful storms, both winter and summer, move in quickly and could strand a man." Mac paused and rubbed his chin. That small gesture clued Nathan into the fact that his client struggled with his conscience. He'd unknowingly and blindly sent his men into dangerous, unfamiliar territory. Twice.

Suddenly, the trees opened up, and the truck slid out of control. The dirt and rock had turned into thick sand in the blink of an eye. Mac cursed and threw the vehicle into four-wheel drive, regaining control faster than Nathan would've thought possible. The dry riverbed spanned what looked to Nathan to be a good hundred yards. Glancing out of the passenger window, he saw the enormity of erosion the river had cut into the land in wetter years.

The thought of trying to cross this waterway when it ran bank to bank had Nathan shaking his head. "I bet this river is a bear to cross when it's running."

Mac laughed. "You'd die if you tried. We're in a wash not a riverbed. There's an enormous difference. This wash flashfloods every time there's a big rain. I've not seen this one flood personally but living in the country and off the land gives me insight. The scary thing is that the weather can be bone dry here but raining somewhere else. You never know when a wall of water might be coming. You'd sure hear it, though. But by that time, it's too late. I'll tell ya', if you've never seen one, flash floods are downright frightening. You don't want to be caught downstream from one. It's an impressive wall of water and debris. In Montana, I've seen them as high as ten-foot tall. By the size of this wash, I can only imagine the height and force of the water as it runs through here. A flash flood is Mother Nature at her most destructive."

Not wanting to think about getting caught in something like that, Nathan redirected the conversation back on point. "Can you tell me what happened with Hank? I don't know him, but he seems like a crusty old coot to me. I wouldn't think much would scare him off."

Mac nodded. "You'd be right. Hank's been with me forever. He was my father's ranch foreman. I'd trust him with my life and have done just that many times. Over the years, that old man has seen more than you could imagine. He's lived his life out on the range. Months at a time, he's slept out in the open with nothing more than a blanket. The last few years I've had to relegate him to the ranch house and let younger men take over the range rides. He's not happy about it, but I'm afraid his aging body can't withstand sitting a horse twelve hours a day anymore.

"I figured if anyone could give me the straight story about what's going on here, it would be Hank. He wanted to get a head start, so he left a day ahead of me." Mac sighed heavily and grumbled in a low whisper, "I should never have let him go alone." After a brief pause, Mac continued. "But that damn old geezer insisted. I think he wanted and planned to tear into the hides of the men that were here before I arrived. Hank doesn't take guff from anyone and demands one hundred percent from our cowboys. As ranch foreman, he was disappointed they'd stopped communicating. He's a tough old cowboy. I'd venture to guess that many of the ranch hands I've hired over the years were and still are afraid of him even at his ripe old age."

Mac became silent, seemingly worrying over whatever had occurred with Hank since he'd arrived yesterday.

"Dammit! One night." Mac's fist slammed down on the steering wheel. "He stayed only one night at the house by himself. You've got to understand Hank's not flighty by any means. Someone got close enough to scare the wits out of him.

"Hank is a practical man. His first priority is *always* his horse. He told me that when he arrived last

20

night, he unloaded the gelding and put him in the corral. Harley, his horse, seemed uneasy, skittish in fact. Hank mentioned something felt off to him too, but he chalked it up to the long drive and being tired—so damn tired that he could hardly keep his eyes open. After making sure the water in the corral was fit to drink and giving his horse some fresh hay, he made his way to the house to bed down for the night.

"Hank's a godly man. Most cowboys are. Not in the sense that they go to church every week, but they do believe in a higher power. Every man that lives out on the range does. You can't be surrounded by all of that beauty and not be affected. I guess you could say the land *is* a cowboy's church."

Mac massaged his temple before continuing. "That crusty old man flinched when he started to tell me about the things he'd witnessed. He said that handmade crosses covered the main house. Twigs, two by fours, you name it, and someone made a cross out of the material. They'd even gone so far as to break up some of the furniture and use that for crosses. They're everywhere—outside, inside, on the doors, on the windows, on the walls, on the staircase. It made him nervous, but at the time he was too tired to give a damn.

"All he could think about was throwing his blanket over a bed and laying his tired butt down. He took his shoes and socks off but didn't even bother to get undressed.

"Sometime during the night, the old man woke up. There was a tapping noise on his window. At first, he thought someone was outside trying to wake him. But since he was on the second story, he figured a tree branch blowing in the wind was more likely the culprit.

It didn't concern him much. He made a mental note to cut the limb in the morning so he wouldn't have that problem again. He rolled over and shut his eyes. Hank told me this because he wanted to make sure I understood that he was awake and not dreaming or sleepwalking when the shit hit the fan.

"Just minutes later, his horse started to squeal. Most people don't know that horses will do that if they're afraid." Mac visibly flinched. "It's a terrible sound.

"Harley started battering and kicking at the fence posts to get out of the corral. The gelding's squeals turned into huffs and frantic neighs. Old Hank said he didn't waste time putting his shoes or socks on and just ran out of the room. But he did remember to grab the long gun he'd left by the bedroom door. Rushing toward the stairs, he took two at a time. Halfway down everything went quiet. The eerie silence was so unexpected it stopped him cold.

"Hank said overwhelming fear paralyzed him and froze the blood in his veins. That's not an easy thing for a man like Hank to admit—even to me. Taking a couple of deep breaths to calm himself, he started to lift his foot to go down another step. Someone rushed him from behind and pushed him down the rest of the stairs. The old man swears he didn't trip. He said he could feel icy hands pressing against his back just before he got shoved. He hit his head several times as he tumbled down the staircase and passed out cold at the bottom. By the time he woke up, the sun was out.

"It took Hank awhile to remember what had happened, but once he did, he ran for the front door." Mac paused. His lips puckered, and his head shook slightly. Nathan felt sure the cowboy was trying to reconcile the bizarre events his ranch foreman had conveyed. Intrigued, Nathan remained on the edge of his seat waiting for the story to unfold.

Mac's shoulders flexed and rolled. "When he made it to the corral, the horse—his friend and companion for years—had a hole in him two feet long and a foot wide. I can't imagine what was going through Hank's mind.

"The old man couldn't make any sense out of what he was seeing. There was *no* blood anywhere. All of the horse's organs, the best he could tell, were gone. The horse's eyes were gouged out. The tongue missing. Old Hank loved that gelding and was devastated by the horse's death. As a cowboy, we deal with animal mortality often, but those mangled remains terrified him.

"Honestly, I don't know what to believe. Hank would never make something like that up. I'm confident we'll know more when we get there. The realtor gave us the name of a vet in St. Johns, the closest town. Hank drove there early this morning to fetch him. The vet's at the corral now trying to figure out what happened.

"Not wanting to stay and knowing I was scheduled to arrive this morning Hank came back out to the ranch turnoff to wait for me. That's where you found us. By the time I reached the edge of the property, he'd worked himself up and decided there was something a little more going on here than what we'd expected.

"I don't believe in the supernatural. Hank never believed in it either. But that old man swore up and down that everything he'd witnessed couldn't be the work of any living man or woman. I'm stymied. Hank's the most down to earth, solid man I've ever known. He's not prone to fits of flightiness."

Taking a few moments to absorb everything Mac had told them, Nathan gathered his wits and queried, "Knowing what you do, what are *your* thoughts on what's going on?"

Mac's jaw tensed, and his barely contained rage became visible in the hardened contours of his face. "Of course, I don't believe it's anything supernatural at all. Whoever did this worked hard to trick poor old Hank. I'm going to kick some serious ass when I find out who's behind all of this. Someone targeting and scaring an old man like that deserves what they get in the way of punishment. I think a little old-fashioned range justice is called for here. Obviously, someone doesn't want me to have this ranch. Over the years I've made enemies. I expect disagreements to be handled man to man. There's going to be hell to pay for whoever is responsible for targeting my men and my ranch."

As Nathan—and he was sure Jursic—chewed on what exactly range justice entailed, an uncomfortable silence took over the rest of the drive.

Chapter Three

Needing some alone time, Bright Flower closed her bedroom door and turned on her bedside lamp. After climbing onto the bed, she reached between the mattress and box spring and pulled out her private journal. Leaning back on the pillows, she opened the book to the next blank page and waited for inspiration.

Since meeting Nathan in person, their dream quests had been different, stronger somehow. They were more alive, less superficial. She thought of their time together in terms of a child playing with paper dolls one day, and the next day, the flimsy material had transformed to three dimensional—flesh and bone. No longer were they stuck at his residence or wherever he fell asleep. From night to night, the landscapes vary. The moon and stars shone more vibrantly, and above all else, everything felt more tangible. Nathan had even asked to learn the Navajo Way, and she was honored to educate him in her beliefs.

During their nightly visits, Bright Flower had recently started teaching Nathan Navajo protocol. Her people would not accept him unless he understood their day-to-day habits. At first, she'd tackled the more straightforward etiquette such as how to greet tribal members, how to handle disputes, the do's and don'ts of everyday living, and so on. These issues may not seem important to most but were imperative when dealing with the traditional members on their reservation.

To date, Bright Flower hadn't shared any of the esoteric rituals of her community, but lately, she'd felt compelled to take her teachings deeper. She'd decided the best way to proceed was to start with basic Navajo history. Once he understood the reach and numbers of her tribe, she'd then go in-depth to one of the most critical Navajo rituals—the Death Ritual. In her estimation, this was the perfect place to start because the tribal beliefs differ so vastly from his culture.

Tapping the pen to her lips, she settled in and let the words write themselves.

Nathan, I want you to know my people, get a feel for them, understand them. To do this, I would like to start with the immensity of our territory. Navajo tribal lands span into three states—Arizona, New Mexico, and Utah. Our reservation is over seventeen million acres garnering the vast region with the distinction of being the largest Native American reservation in the United States.

My people are profoundly religious and live their lives traditionally. As I've said before in our dreams, our history is steeped in taboo. There is no separation between our spiritualism and daily lives. That being the case, tribesmen seek out my services as a tribal singer—more commonly known to outsiders as medicine men and women, or shamans. It is my duty to provide everything from healing the sick to presiding over and performing ceremonies. The Navajo people have many joyous occasions that we celebrate through rituals such as The Blessing Way for the birth of a child, or The Sun Dance, which marks the summer solstice just to name a few.

My grandfather and I are highly sought out for our abilities as singers and are visited often by tribesmen from other states. As singers, we are exceptionally skilled, but that is not the sole reason people come to us. Spirit Keeper and I were born high witches who are adept at practicing Navajo magic. The gift of native witchcraft is passed through our genes from generation to generation. This subject, I'm afraid, is a lesson all unto itself for which we will discuss at another time.

By far, the Navajo death rituals are the most important ceremonies performed by singers. There can be no deviation while executing the end of life rituals. Otherwise, the consequences to the tribesmen would be devastating. At this critical juncture in the Navajo community, I am the barrier between them and the spirit world—their only source of protection. Unlike Europeans, my people have a deep-seated fear of spirits. Even those visitations from beloved family members, which the majority of people in the modern world crave, are perceived by my tribesmen as a terrifying sign of evil doings. Our legend states that if a tribal member comes into contact with a spirit—any spirit—death will find them within four days. So, ghosts are to be avoided at all costs. This conviction is neither a good belief nor bad. It is simply the way of my people.

****

With the morning chores done and Nathan's evening tutorial firmly outlined, Bright Flower whipped up a cup of her special-blended herbal tea and sat on the front steps of the house trailer to enjoy a few moments of sunshine.

A slight smirk crossed her lips when the image of Martin—the newest in the lengthy line of husband candidates—was sent packing. If only Grandfather would just listen to the truth. Life would be so much easier.

The breeze picked up and a flash of color caught her attention. An Indian Paintbrush wildflower had inexplicably appeared at the base of the stairs. Picking the posy, she twirled the deep orange bloom between her fingers, and couldn't resist sniffing the familiar fragrance. The scent was neither sweet nor pungent. The perfume held the promise of a fertile, wild prairie and soothed her spirit. Late February was far too early for the sprig to bloom naturally. But the Creator had offered the gift, and she'd happily accept the flower as a good omen. If ever she needed one, it was now.

While Bright Flower and Spirit Keeper had recently been at odds, she'd noticed today that her grandfather was not well. Not that he would ever admit such a weakness to her. There was no fever, no sign of sickness at all. Try as she might, she couldn't grasp what the problem was, but the elder's eyes looked dull somehow as if the shine of life's vigor was starting to falter. That scared her. The elder had always been so vital, so alert. She cursed herself for allowing anger to blind her to her grandfather's wellbeing. This insight left her wondering if that might be the crux responsible for the sudden never-ending urgency of her marital status.

Contemplating the healing ceremony she planned for Spirit Keeper, with or without his permission, Bright Flower leaned back against the steps on her elbows and opened herself up to the surroundings. The pull of the earth's magic would certainly guide her in the right direction. Large, puffy, cotton ball clouds lazily made their way across the light blue sky. Over the years, she'd gained great spiritual insight while gazing at the heavens. She crossed her fingers and hoped for more showers. If only she could bottle the smell of rain as it fell and quenched the earth's thirst.

A deafening rumble from ill-running engines traveling far too fast down the dirt road broke the silence of the moment. Several vehicles, some towing livestock trailers, came to an abrupt halt in front of Bright Flower's home. Once the doors opened and the occupants started filing out, Bright Flower recognized several of her Navajo tribesmen and women from New Mexico. They'd traveled from the farthest eastern region of the reservation.

Before any of them could speak, their sorrow slapped her senses. The healing work she had planned for Spirit Keeper would have to be put on hold. There was only one reason an entire family would show up unannounced at her doorstep. Someone was dying—or worst-case scenario—already dead.

Standing, Bright Flower dropped the Creator's gifted bloom into her breast pocket and nodded at the crowd. She fixed her gaze on a man who had stepped forward.

"Yá'át'ééh." The elder raised his hand but didn't offer a smile.

"Yá'át'ééh." Bright Flower scanned the group in front of her and, thankfully, didn't pick up on any lingering dead. "Is your loved one still among the earth people, or has he already passed into the spirit world?"

Navajo men were proud and under normal

circumstances never showed fear. It was apparent in the way this tribesman shifted his weight from foot to foot that he was more than a little uneasy. "We were afraid we wouldn't make it in time. With each hour that passes, he travels farther from the living. He is still breathing but doesn't have much time left. My family is nervous. I beg of you. We must work fast."

Tilting her head and pointing her nose toward the earthen structure fifty yards to the east, Bright Flower instructed, "Take him to the healing hogan. Place him on the bed within and light the fire in the center pit first. Once that is done, you must light the blaze outside beside the lean-to. I will be along in just a moment." Not waiting for a reply, she pivoted and disappeared into the trailer to grab her medicine bag and drum.

****

All eyes were upon Bright Flower as she strode at a quick clip to the hogan. As expected, the majority of friends and family lingered outside the confines of the mud walls. Their fear of the dead and dying was far too great to enter the healing hut. As she approached, they bowed their heads with respect and stepped back. Before turning her attention to the outdoor fire, she queried, "Which two will dig the grave?"

Two young men stepped forward—their heads still bowed. A tightness formed in Bright Flower's chest, and she could feel the creases of concern form between her eyes. She didn't have time for this but considering the boys' ages she was duty bound to question them. "You are both terribly young. Do you have experience with preparing a grave and participating in the burial ceremony?"

"Yes," they answered in unison.

The family surely knew the dangers of the death ritual to both the living and dead. Bright Flower had to believe that these young men had studied and adequately trained for their duties. There was no time to question them any further. "Okay. Follow the path going north away from the hogan. Do not stray from the trail. In the event there are any wandering spirits, you will be protected if you stick to the path. A gravesite has been preselected, marked, and blessed at the end of the trail. That is where you will dig." As much as she hated to prepare ahead, sometimes there wasn't any time to do what needed to be done before a family arrived.

She waited for their nods of agreement before continuing. "For the safety of those closest to me, do not stop short. You *must* travel the full length of the trail and dig at the place I have preselected. When you are finished, return as fast as you are able. For your protection, take a seat on the east side of the hogan and wait for further instruction. You will be needed to complete the ceremony so make haste." The young men grabbed their shovels and jogged off into the horizon.

"The rest of you will find shelter in another hogan over there." Again, she tilted her head high into the air to point them in the right direction. "Do not stray from the structure. Please make yourselves comfortable but remain silent. Once the spirit has left the body, we do not want him to dwell. If you heed my words, all will be well."

The outdoor fire was in full blaze. Bright Flower set her bag down and began sorting out everything she would need. Once she was ready, she stood in front of the roaring fire pit offering herself up to the spirit world. She was proud to serve her community by giving members of her tribe these last rites. Even though powerful Navajo magic protected her, she called on the strength of the warrior that every Navajo carried within themselves. Bright Flower's body shivered as the force of the bravery of her ancestors enveloped her and gave her the strength to face down the supernatural on behalf of a beloved tribesman.

With closed eyes, Bright Flower tilted her head back, and focused on the sound of cedar resin crackling within the fire. The lively sparks of the flames formed on the back of her eyelids and danced skyward elevating her own spirit higher and higher. The dense smoke filled her lungs and purified her body.

The Holy One's power, slight at first, suddenly burst throughout Bright Flower filling her earthly vessel with light. The raw energy shocked her system sending trembles throughout her body. Just as the force of the mighty Colorado River slices a trail through the Grand Canyon or the bull elk's shrill majestic bugle cuts through the air, she was now a part of nature—no longer a mere mortal being. She was a part of *all* things. Her spirit animal, the eagle, screeched its approval as it soared above.

Feeling light as a feather, Bright Flower concentrated on the soil beneath her feet. Her mind pictured strong, solid roots growing through her lower limbs. Each stem burrowed deep into the red dirt. For protection from specters, she must stay tethered to Mother Earth. Otherwise, in this altered state, those that wander in the ether might confuse her with a phantom and carry her off into the depths of the Underworld.

Bright Flower raised her arms skyward to seek out

the Creator's counsel. Through ancient song, she requested the holy presence as a safety barrier between her soul as well as any other living beings that would have direct contact with the soon to be deceased. Warm tingles tickled the tips of her fingers and swiftly moved down her body signifying the protection was indeed in place.

Satisfied that all personal safety measures for the dangers of dealing with the spirit world had been observed Bright Flower got busy. She tossed a specific combination of blessed local flora into the flame. It would serve to repel evil spirits that would try to take advantage of family members participating in the death ritual. The blaze flared and devoured the dried plants, sending a dense, light gray smoke spiraling into the air. Once the flames calmed, she reached in with a shovel and filled a large cast iron pot with ash. Setting the blackened powdered cinders aside to cool ensured she wouldn't be treating burns after the ceremony had concluded.

Time was of the essence. The heat almost knocked Bright Flower over when she stepped inside the healing hogan. The discomfort couldn't be helped. The blaze in the center of the earthen floor was necessary in order to banish any unclean and harmful spirits that may be hiding within the shelter. Bright Flower scattered more of the blessed dried plants over the flames, and then squatted in front of the purifying fire. Placing the sacred drum squarely on her lap, she began the sorrowful call to the Creator on behalf of the dying. The deep resonance of each beat traveled up her arm and reverberated throughout her soul. Haunting ancient chants and song floated on the air.

Springing to her feet, Bright Flower bent over to inspect the old man. His breathing faltered, indicating that his remaining time with the earth people was short. They'd have to work fast to prepare him for the spirit world. Without removing her eyes from the elder, she shouted commands to the two men who waited close by for additional instruction. "Go to the fire outside. I've placed protective ash into a pot. Remove your clothing and cover your bodies with the powder. It will shield you from the spirit world as your grandfather passes over. Return to this room only wearing your moccasins." As the men were leaving, she directed, "Be fast."

Bright Flower hated rushing through her chants, but time was of the essence. The elder had to be moved outside of the healing hogan before he died. If he took his last breath within the confines of the mud hut, they'd have to knock the north wall out immediately so his spirit would be free to move on. Then, after the burial, the remaining shell of the hogan must be destroyed and a new one built in a different location. Otherwise, anyone entering would be in danger from the spirit world.

Inwardly she sighed in relief when the ash-covered men returned in time. Bright Flower's tightly wound muscles unclenched and relaxed a bit. "Carry him to the cot in front of the flame outside." The men gently picked their relative up and moved him where she directed. Once outside, she noticed that the personal items to be buried with the body were placed neatly on a handmade wooden table. A supple doeskin pouch slouched beside them. As Bright Flower carefully filled the small bag with her tribesman's possessions, she glanced around for the elder's horse.

Worried that the animal may have escaped, she inquired, "Where have you tied his horse?"

With eyes downcast, one of the men closed the distance between them and spoke in a reverent whisper. "Grandfather was an active man throughout his life. He was bedridden for most of the last year. I understand that it goes against all tradition, but he requested his horse stay with the earth people as he made his journey into the spirit world on foot. Being denied the use of his legs this last year, he wanted the freedom to walk to the Underworld."

Bright Flower's gasp caught in her throat as she moved to within inches of the naked man. Rage flared at the thought that these family members would condone such an act of sacrilege. Her reply was harsh and hissed through clenched teeth. "No. His horse must accompany him. If he were to *walk* in spirit form to the Underworld, too many earth people would be in jeopardy. I insist that his horse make the journey with him. It is the way of things."

The man raised his head. Sorrowful eyes locked onto hers trying to persuade her. "But…" Angry over the defiance, her icy glare cut him off. *If grandfather were presiding this man would never be so disrespectful.*

"If your family fails to adhere to the traditional death ceremony, I insist that you take your grandfather and leave now. The danger would be yours and your family's alone. I refuse to unleash a roving spirit onto unsuspecting innocents."

Fear had him taking a step back and lowering his head. "His horse shall make the journey with him."

Bright Flower took a deep breath and allowed the anger to subside. Knowing the man was only trying to follow his grandfather's wishes—as absurd as they were—she gently placed her hand on his shoulder for comfort. "Please stand at the foot of the cot." Turning to address the other man, she encouraged, "If you would stand at the head of the cot, I will continue the prayers."

After adding embers from the fire pit to the smudge pot which held the remaining ash the men had dusted on their bodies, Bright Flower started singing. An eagle feather waved the smoke over the old man's body for the first part of the cleansing process preparing him for the journey ahead. The end was near.

Before the elder could take his last breath, Bright Flower filled another pot with clean water. Setting it on the floor next to the cot, she spoke with urgency, "Any moment now it will be time for you to bathe your grandfather. Once done, dress him in his best clothing. Place the left moccasin on his right foot and the right moccasin on his left. Wrap his body in the blanket you've brought for him.

"Once death has come, no one must speak or utter a sound. Doing so would confuse the spirit. He may not believe he is dead and could follow you home. Shed no tears. Doing so bewilders the spirit, and he will not make the journey to the Underworld. All ties to this world must be severed at once." The men solemnly nodded their understanding.

A loud gurgling gasp interrupted Bright Flower's instructions. Stepping beside the cot, she recognized the death stare. The elder had died. Pivoting, she nodded her head toward the basin of water and left the men to do their duty.

The boys sent to dig the grave had returned, and she found them sitting quietly beside the hogan. Putting her finger to her lips, she signified that the time had come. They rose in unison and took their places.

****

Almost an hour had passed when the two men signaled their readiness to begin the journey to the grave. One of the boys took the horse by the reins. The elder's possessions accompanying him into the spirit world were tied carefully onto the back of the pony. The silent journey to the freshly dug grave began.

The first boy started down the path. Since talking was not allowed, he was resigned to using sign language to warn anyone wandering the area to take heed—their grandfather's spirit was near.

The second boy tugged on the reins of the sacrificial horse and headed out. The two older men positioned the deceased on their shoulders and started the final journey with their loved one. Bright Flower followed behind, carrying a freshly cut piñon branch.

The journey to the grave was slow and silent. Even the abundant wildlife residing in the area took heed and disappeared when a spirit had been set free from the body.

Bright Flower remained a good fifty feet behind the procession. Her attention was riveted to the two men as they carefully placed the securely wrapped body in the freshly dug grave. By the time she reached the burial site, they had arranged the personal items on top of their deceased. Handfuls of earth covered the elder. Once the grave was filled completely the young boy handed the horse's reins over to one of the ash-covered men. Both boys rushed back to the safety of the hogan. The horse was dispatched and left lying next to the buried body. The men took their leave, but Bright Flower's duties were not yet over. Her hands rose to the sky as she silently implored, *'Creator, show this elder the ways of the spirit. Help him journey safely to the outstretched arms of his ancestors in the Underworld.'*

Circling the grave and then the horse, she used the piñon cutting to obscure all signs of footprints left behind in the loose dirt. This process ensured the spirit would not become confused and follow the tracks back to his family. Walking backward, she continued this chore the entire length of the pathway to the healing hogan.

By the time her obligatory tasks had been fulfilled, and she arrived back at the mud hut the family had long since gone. The only sign they'd been there was a lone sheep tied to the healing hogan as compensation for her services. The corners of her lips curled in a faint smile as she thought about walking home with her payment. Over the years, being paid in the traditional manner had become less frequent. As of late, Bright Flower's services were rewarded out of the family's hard-earned money. Since she didn't have a materialistic bone in her body, taking money for spiritual services was not a priority. While she appreciated the fact that her people wanted to compensate her with cold hard cash, she still preferred payment in the form of sheep. The animals were compensation that kept giving back to her tribe for years. The wool sheared from the bodies of the bartered livestock produced softer yarn after the spinning process. When dyed, the colors were richer and more vibrant than the wool harvested from her personal sheep. The blankets she'd made with the special fiber were highly sought after and brought an elevated price that she willingly gifted back into her community. She believed this was so because of the nature from which she'd received the animal.

After dousing the remaining fire in both pits, she and her sheep journeyed back to the trailer. Her eyelids fluttered from exhaustion. In her weakened state, her limbs didn't feel strong enough to carry her another step. Utterly spent, she released the animal in a small pasture, pivoted, and focused on each stride to keep from falling over.

Spirit Keeper was sleeping on the couch so Bright Flower tiptoed to her room doing her best to miss the squeaky parts of the floor. Too exhausted to hold herself up any longer, she crumpled onto the bed and allowed a long sigh of relief to escape. It had been a long grueling day. It mattered not how her work drained her physically and mentally—she would never give it up. Without the old ways, she would be lost. Her beloved people would be lost.

Tugging the now wilted Indian Paintbrush from deep inside her blouse pocket, Bright Flower gently cradled the bloom. Closing her eyes, and as usual, her thoughts drifted to Nathan. She'd never doubted that he was a huge part of her life. *It simply was.* She'd never questioned that the Creator had chosen him as her husband. *It simply was.* The gifted bloom encouraged her that all things would work out in time.

She and Nathan had walked through the land of dreams together joined by Bright Flower's spirit animal, the eagle. Many times, they'd ridden together through the misty dreamscape on the back of Nathan's buffalo spirit animal. Her eagle was just as smitten with his buffalo as the woman was with the man.

Nathan's face was rounded perfectly for cupping between her hands. The thought inspired a sleepy grin. While he didn't currently sport a beard, he had in the past, at least in her dreams. She liked the facial hair. Most Native American men have soft facial hair that is not conducive to full beards. Nathan's brown hair held just a touch of red which matched the color of an elk's mane. Rubbing her fingertips together provoked the fond memory of brushing his hair from his eyes. Bright Flower softly moaned as she thought of Nathan's beautiful, soft, caramel-colored eyes full of love and promises.

As each day went by, it was getting harder and harder to hold Spirit Keeper and his proposed marriage suitors at bay. Since the elder had heard no word from Nathan, Bright Flower's power of persuasion over Spirit Keeper dwindled in regard to each new match that came along. Soon Grandfather would make a match, any match, without her consent.

The Creator had spoken. Nathan was *her* man, and she would believe that until her last breath. Giving herself to anyone else would be dishonest. Bright Flower had to keep reminding herself that her grandfather pushed the subject of marriage out of fear. Fear for her future. *I beg of you, Holy one, please send Spirit Keeper a vision of what's to come. Help him see what you've already made clear to me.*

Rolling over and burying her head into the pillow, Bright Flower allowed the bone-deep weariness to overtake her as the vision of Nathan's face slowly faded into sleep.

Chapter Four

Nathan, Jursic, and Mac pulled up to the ranch house just as a young man wearing filthy, torn jeans shut the back panel to a trailer. Nathan didn't miss the Smith and Wesson holstered on his left side with the grip facing out for easy access. Hell, the gun was just as big as its wearer. Even though the stranger didn't appear to be a threat, he made a mental note to be aware of where the kid was at all times. Other people carrying sidearms made him nervous—especially those he didn't know. There was no sign of the vet.

When the boy turned to greet them, he was much older than Nathan had initially thought.

The three of them quickly piled out of the truck. Mac held his hand out and made the introductions. "I'm Mac. I own this ranch. These men are Nathan and Jursic. Where can we find the vet?"

The young man wiped his hands on his jeans before accepting Mac's greeting and smirked. "That would be me." Sensing their surprise, the veterinarian apologized while shaking everyone's hands. "I assure you that I don't normally look this bad. I had an emergency last night and had just gotten back this morning when Hank pulled up. He was so distraught I didn't think it would be prudent to take the time to shower and change. That's why I'm so grungy."

Surprisingly, the slightly built man's handshake was firm and confident. If the rough calluses were any indicator, the man was used to some pretty hard labor and hid his small framed muscles well.

"Pleased to meet you all. I'm Vern, the new large animal vet in St. Johns. I'm sorry we have to meet under these circumstances. I had to tear down a few of your corral posts to position the tractor to retrieve the horse. I hope you don't mind, but I didn't see any way around it."

Mac waved him off to show he understood. "I appreciate you coming all the way out here on such short notice."

"As you can see, I've just finished loading the tractor. The horse is on the front of the trailer and ready to go back to town."

Nathan's ears perked up when he heard a faint whimper. Seemingly oblivious to the sound, the other men continued their conversation. He scoured the area to no avail for whatever was responsible for making the noise.

Returning his attention to the discussion, Nathan watched as Mac quickly surveyed the empty corral. "Can you tell us what happened here? My foreman was a little shaky on the details of the injuries."

Vern scrutinized Mac before he answered, his demeanor turning serious. "I can understand why. They were...well, for now, let's just say that the wounds were unusual. I've never seen the equal of traumatic injuries to any other animal. Right off the top of my head, I can't explain what caused them." Glancing at the now empty corral, Vern scratched his chin. "I'm not positive, mind you, but the wounds were so horrific, they looked…" Stopping in mid-sentence, the vet grimaced.

He has something on his mind but isn't comfortable saying it out loud, Nathan thought.

Mac's eyes zeroed in on Vern and squinted, trying to will the man to continue. When he didn't, he finally queried, "They looked like *what*?"

The vet's left hand rested on the butt of his pistol. After a deep sigh, he looked at the tree line in the distance. "Ritualistic. I can't swear by it, but if you want my first impression, *that's* the only thing that comes to mind."

Nathan couldn't help himself. He had to find out how qualified this man was before he took anything he said as gospel. "How *long* have you been a vet?"

Vern smiled as if he were in on an inside joke. "If that's a roundabout way to ask my age, I'm thirty-three. I know I look young, but I've been doing this for about ten years now. I grew up on a ranch and have seen just about every kind of animal injury and death you could imagine. So, I've got plenty of experience under my belt. When I say I've *never* seen these types of injuries before, *that's* saying something."

The vet pivoted to speak directly to Mac. "I have to ask, are there any other animals on this ranch?" The man's concern was thinly veiled.

Mac shook his head as he released a heavy sigh. Nathan recognized the rancher's frustration. He didn't believe a man like John MacAllister settled for anything other than complete and utter control over any situation life threw at him. "I'm sorry, but I just don't know the answer to that question. I *had* men here. They brought their own horses. I haven't had any contact with them in a while now. That's why I'm here. I *can* tell you there are no cattle yet, and none will make the trip until I know they won't be brutalized or butchered."

Vern nodded as he listened. "Before I loaded the horse on the trailer, I took pictures." Pulling his phone out, he handed it over to Mac. Nathan and Jursic positioned themselves on either side of the rancher to glimpse the gruesome photos.

"I'm taking the carcass to my facility where I can do a proper necropsy. You'll notice that the injuries are extensive and there is no blood to be found anywhere in the corral or surrounding area. It's as if the wound was somehow instantaneously cauterized as the injuries were being inflicted. Even then, I can't imagine how there wouldn't be even one drop of blood."

Nathan's focus shifted back to the vet. He pulled a card out and handed it to Vern. "Please send me all of the pictures you took along with any findings of the necropsy. I'm a little out of my element when it comes to animals. I don't know how in-depth a necropsy is, but I'd appreciate it if you ran some drug tests. Your findings could help point us in a direction to look for the perpetrator."

Vern nodded. "Of course. It'll take some time, but I'll send you everything I find. I have to tell you that right now, I'm stumped. I'm the only large animal vet in St. Johns which means my time is spread pretty thin, but I plan to make this a priority. If I don't find anything through research, I may call my father. He might have some insight into whatever could've done this." Mystified, he smacked his lips and shook his head. "Hopefully, I'll have some solid answers for you in a week or so."

Questions littered Nathan's mind. "About the wounds, can you venture a guess as to what type of weapon may have caused them?"

The younger man steadfastly shook his head. "No. I *can* tell you that it looks like something went clean through that animal." Scratching his head, he finally just shrugged. "There are no torn edges on the wounds. Whatever happened, it must have occurred quickly, because I don't see any animal standing still while that was done to them."

"Okay. You'd said before that you've been a veterinarian for the last ten years and that you were new to the area. Is there another vet in the surrounding area that we can consult with?"

"No. I'm afraid not. I'm the only vet around these parts. Gallup, New Mexico, is about forty or fifty miles up the main road from here. But I'm not aware of any New Mexico vets servicing this area."

"Where can we find the last veterinarian?"

"That would be Mark Carson. I'm afraid you'd find him in the St. Johns Catholic Cemetery. He died a short time before I arrived. The town put a notice out requesting a resident large animal vet. That's how I came here and acquired his practice. I'm new to this area and haven't gotten my feet under me yet. I've met most of the ranchers, but to the best of my knowledge, no one has had anything like this happen on their land. If they have, they've kept it a secret from me. I'll be happy to go through Dr. Carson's files. Maybe he has something in his notes that will shed some light on this."

A low keening yelp turned into a deep growl. Nathan jumped and spun around to face the truck. "Did anyone else hear that? Where is that sound coming from?"

Vern placed his hand on Nathan's elbow, probably to calm him. "That's my dog. He's been hunkered down on the floorboard since we got on the property. He refuses to come out. He's terrified. That's the reason I'm carrying my gun. I've got to tell you after seeing what happened here, I've been *real* careful to watch my back."

Looking a trifle impatient Mac spoke up, "Thank you, Vern. I appreciate anything you can tell us about the cause of death. We'll all be looking forward to your reports. There's a lot of ground to cover this afternoon, so we've got to get a move on."

****

The men wandered around and through the corral looking for any sign that might shed some light on the horse's death. Mac found some skin and smatterings of blood on the wooden railings—probably where the animal had tried to escape prior to being killed. But other than that, there was nothing to show what had taken place.

Nathan shifted his focus to the main house. While the sun shone brightly, the structure seemed dull somehow as if it were under a perpetual shadow. It was clear that no one had lived here for decades. The house itself registered high on the creepy scale. Appreciation for old Hank's iron will elevated. *There's no way in hell I'd spend a night here.*

A bright flash caught Nathan's interest and drew him closer to the ranch house. Shielding his eyes to get a better look, a crudely fashioned tin cross hanging on the outside of the second story between two windows glittered. Unease prickled at the back of his neck and every muscle tensed. A lump formed squarely in the pit of his midsection causing instant nausea. He could only imagine the desperation someone must've felt to go to all the trouble of adding a religious icon in such a precarious position. *Someone had to be scared out of their minds to do such a thing.* Lost in thought, Nathan almost jumped out of his skin when he was bumped from behind. Spinning around, he drew his weapon without thinking twice.

Jursic's hands flew high into the air. "Whoa! It's me. What's wrong?"

Doing his best to calm the jitters, Nathan forced his arm to relax and re-holstered the gun. "We have to clear the house." Shouting his intentions out to Mac, who was still searching the corral, he stated in no uncertain terms, "To be on the safe side Jursic and I are going inside. I want you to stay back until we call you in."

Mac started to protest, but this was why they were hired. Nathan wouldn't take any guff from the client. "Let us do our job. Once the house is deemed safe, I want you to come in and tell me if you notice anything amiss." Reluctantly, Mac nodded his agreement and made his way to the vehicle to wait. Once there he motioned to Jursic.

Nathan slid his gaze back to the front of the house. He'd wait for his partner before going inside.

Jursic made enough noise walking back to Nathan so that he didn't pull his gun again. His partner handed him a walkie talkie. "Mac said to keep these on us. Since there's no cell service, it's the only way to communicate here."

Clipping the radio to his hip, they tested the

strength of each porch step before moving on to the next. Nathan would rather be anywhere else right now. His breathing turned laborious, and his heartbeat thumped off the charts. *If it were up to me, I'd burn this place to the fucking ground and never look back.* But it wasn't up to him. Chewing the inside of his cheek, he forcefully pushed back at his raw nerves.

Pulling his gun, Jursic whispered, "I feel like I'm in a slasher movie. I count…" he paused for a moment. "Holy shit, man, there are thirteen crosses on the front porch alone. What the hell is *that* all about?"

"Beats me but be ready for anything. I'm quickly coming around to Hank's way of thinking. *Something* is going on here that isn't easily explained away."

Jursic's cheek biting and nervous throat clearing would have been laughable if Nathan hadn't felt the exact same way. "Well, shit," his partner exclaimed on a shaky breath.

"If it helps—ditto. Welcome to the private sector, Jursic." He offered a bright grin for his friend. "There's never a dull moment. It's time to get serious. I'll take the downstairs. You go upstairs. Check every nook and cranny. I want to hear you clear every room before you move on to the next. I'll do the same down here. I don't want any surprises."

"You got it, man. And Nathan?"

"Yeah?"

"Aim for the head. Don't waste your time shooting body mass."

Confused, Nathan felt the creases in his forehead deepening. "What?"

"Zombies don't die unless you shoot them in the head. I'm not sure why but their brain—or what's left of it—has to be hit."

Staring quizzically at Jursic with a raised eyebrow, Nathan rolled his eyes. "You're an idiot."

Feigning offense, his friend quipped, "Don't look at me like that. Since I met you and your friends a year ago, we've dealt with ghosts, witches, and demons. In my book, that makes zombies the next logical progression. It's best not to take any chances. Head shot."

Nathan snickered. "Really? Are you seriously quoting grade B movies to me at a time like this? Dude, you've got to get a life."

"Look, man, I've gotta tell ya', I feel as though I've walked right into a scene from a horror flick, and not one of the spoofs, either. The freak flag is flying high and proud today, brother."

He didn't argue. The vibe surrounding this place was downright disturbing.

Jursic was on a roll. "After the last disaster we went through at Terry's house, nothing going on around here would surprise me. I'm telling you man, zombies." Starting to enjoy himself, Jursic leaned on the doorframe as if they had all the time in the world. "You know, we should consider changing the name of the company from Bastion Enterprises to Spooks-Or-Us."

Nathan recognized that his friend's humor was a stall tactic. They were both evading the problem at hand. "Are you done?"

"Or maybe something more along the lines of Specter Annihilators. Yeah. I like—"

Nathan's hand shot out and thumped Jursic on the chest. "Can it. I'm not sure I want to go in either, but it's our job. The client is watching us. We've wasted enough time. Let's get this done."

"You got it, boss man."

Nathan jerked on the old screen door and wasn't surprised in the least when it creaked and shuddered. Glancing at his friend he grinned. "So much for a surprise attack."

Jursic raised his weapon and tapped his head. "Zombies have excellent hearing. I'm telling you, shoot for the noggin, man."

Nathan breached the doorway fast and low, moving right. Jursic flew up the stairs yelling, "Head shot! Head shot!" Nathan couldn't help but chuckle. Not only was his friend a highly qualified ex-cop—an essential in their line of business—but he was always good for a laugh. At tense times like this, that was an excellent quality to have around.

Chapter Five

"Come on in." Once again, the old screen door protested with a nerve-grating screech as Nathan opened it wide for Mac.

"What did you find?"

Nathan turned to his friend. "Jursic, why don't you start with the upstairs? Anything out of the norm up there?"

Jursic's mouth puckered. The effect was a bit like a fish trying to breathe on land. "Well, I found suitcases under beds. The drawers were full of clothes. The bathrooms had toiletries scattered around. It doesn't look like anything has been disturbed or used for a couple of weeks, though. There's a layer of dust on everything."

At this point, nothing surprised Nathan. Holding his hand out to guide the men, he stated, "Let's go into the kitchen. I want to show you something."

Passing through the swinging door, they found plates on the table caked with dried food. Brewed coffee had molded in the pot. Nathan opened the refrigerator door and covered his nose from the foul stench of rotting food. "I can't be sure, but it looks like your men just picked up and left in the middle of breakfast. I don't know what to think about all of this. To say the least, it's troubling."

Showing just how tired and perplexed he was, Mac rubbed his face. Deeply creased lines stood out with what Nathan perceived as fatigue. He had to remind himself that coupled with worry over his men the rancher had spent hours cooped up in his truck driving straight through from Montana. Mac had to be on his last leg. "I found one of the four-wheelers I sent with my ranch hands. I put a jug of water in the backseat. Let's jump in and take a quick run out to the range cabin. It's about fifteen miles north of here. Maybe one or more of them are hurt and holed up there."

"Are you sure you're up to doing that today? Maybe we should go back to Flagstaff and come back Monday after you've had some rest." Nathan knew he'd made a fatal error when Mac grabbed his shirt collar and jerked him close.

"My men could be hurt out there. I'm not going to rest until I've checked. You can come with me, or you can stay behind." Each word was laced with unconcealed anger.

"You're right. Of course. We'll go with you. Just give us one minute to get our coats out of the truck."

Mac released his hold on Nathan, whirled around, and stormed out of the room without another word.

Trying to be the voice of reason, Jursic piped up. "Nathan, I'm not sure about doing this today. It's already noon. We've got a long drive back to Flagstaff. We promised we'd be back tonight. And besides that, there's no way in hell I want to get stranded anywhere on this property."

"Yeah. I feel the same way. But you heard the man. He won't leave until he can check on his men. He's right. They could be hurt or worse. I made a promise to

Hank that I intend to keep. Under the circumstances, I can't be sure it's safe here. Going with Mac is the only chance we've got to convince him to come back to Flagstaff with us and gather reinforcements. Until then, we're out of options.

"Come on. While Mac's driving us to the cabin, we'll have to figure out the best way to reason with him. I don't want to be put in the position of dragging him off of the property forcefully."

The all-terrain vehicle roared to life as Nathan hopped into the front bucket seat and Jursic jumped into the back. Reaching above his head to grab the roll bar, Nathan glanced over his shoulder and scanned the house one last time as they drove by.

The dilapidated building refused to give up any secrets or clues. But what in blue blazes could have happened to Mac's men, not to mention Hank's horse? Even if it was caused by supernatural occurrences, surely there was a reason.

Nathan was deep in thought when the four-wheeler suddenly jerked to a stop. He flew forward and smacked his forehead on the windshield resulting in an instant piercing headache. Clutching his head, Nathan yelled, "Dammit! What did you do tha—" But Mac was out of the vehicle with his six-shooter drawn before he could finish the question.

Jursic and Nathan quickly followed suit, flanking their client. Crouching low and drawing their weapons, Jursic scanned left, and Nathan scrutinized everything to the right. Doing his best to keep the sting of concern from his voice, Nathan whispered, "What's wrong? Did you see someone?"

"No. Look at that."

Pivoting, Nathan studied his client. Mac's face was unreadable, but the man's eyes reflected outright disbelief. Following the rancher's line of sight, Nathan's gaze fell upon a water trough. As far as he could see, there was nothing unusual about the large vessel. It looked to be a standard, everyday watering container for livestock. He'd remembered seeing another one just like it inside of the corral. *Why would they have a livestock watering station where they parked their vehicles?* He had to admit that it didn't make sense. But then again, he wasn't a rancher. Nathan hadn't noticed it on the way in, but why would he?

Mac stood at his full height and bellowed, "Who's out there?" His booming voice held no fear, only rage. Nathan and Jursic maintained their defensive stance slowly surveying every visible nook and cranny for any threat. "I'll find you bastards, and we'll settle this once and for all. Show yourselves, dammit!"

A few moments of uncomfortable silence passed before Mac holstered his weapon. Unsure about what had led the rancher to believe they weren't alone, Nathan and Jursic continued to scan the tree line around the house and corral while holding their sidearms high.

"You might as well put your weapons away. Whoever did this are cowards. They're not about to show themselves." The rancher inched forward studying the ground around the trough. His gaze bobbed back and forth between the corral and large water basin.

Stumped, Nathan questioned, "Did what? *What* makes you believe there is someone close by?"

"This water trough has been moved. It must've

happened when we were in the house. Whoever did this didn't spill a drop of water and left no sign of how they moved it." Mac scratched his chin and shook his head. "How in the world did they manage this?" The words, a mere whisper, were spoken under his breath, disbelief bleeding through. Nathan was positive the rancher's incredulous question wasn't meant for them to hear. But the cowboy's adrenaline was ramped up, resulting in him speaking louder than he thought.

Sidling up to the full trough, Mac bent over and grunted with the effort of trying to lift the water basin. It didn't budge. Nathan and Jursic joined the rancher. They grasped the lip of the trough, and all of them heaved at the same time. The damn thing was so heavy that their efforts didn't even slosh the water inside.

Jursic looked a bit spooked. "You must be wrong. There is no way someone could've moved this. The trough is full to the top and has got to weigh at least a thousand pounds or more. Not only would water have spilled over, but we would have *heard* something."

"I am *not* out of my mind. Follow me." Mac spun around and entered the corral. Once reaching the farthest railing, he gestured to the ground. "Take a look at that." There right in front of them was a clear imprint of where the trough had been. Examining the loose dirt in the area, Nathan found no footprints, no tracks from any vehicle, and no clues as to what had occurred. There was no sign that the heavy load had been dragged. The only thing that was completely clear was that it appeared as though the trough had been lifted straight up off of the ground. The hair on the nape of Nathan's neck stood on end. Casually rubbing the affected area, he scoured the surroundings. There was no sign of a single living soul, and yet he felt eyes—predatory eyes—boring into him from every direction.

Removing the phone from his pocket, he snapped pictures for his files. He had a terrible feeling that this was just the first of many oddly shaped puzzle pieces before the bigger picture came into focus.

****

Even with the state-of-the-art four-wheeler, it took forever to cross the rugged landscape. Just guessing, Nathan thought they'd traveled about twelve or thirteen miles, but they were crawling along at a snail's pace. The farther they breached the land, the rougher the going. Mac suddenly veered the vehicle to the right to miss another large boulder bulging from the earth. The four-wheeler didn't quite clear the obstacle completely, and a .30-30 lever action long gun, resting between the bucket seats, worked its way free. The stock of the rifle rammed into Nathan's ribs causing a sharp flash of pain.

"Sorry about that." Without seemingly giving it an extra thought, Mac grabbed the gun and tucked it securely back beside him—never taking his eyes from the path they were driving on. Nathan grunted and slid his hand inside his coat to rub the throbbing pain.

Throughout the past several hours, the once gentle breeze had grown colder and stronger. Dense, dark clouds now consumed the sky, and were a sure sign they were about to be hit with a late winter storm. Any hopeful chance of the afternoon sun keeping them warm had been obliterated. Considering how short the February days were, at this rate, they'd never make it back to the safety of the truck before nightfall.

With teeth rattling from the latest chilly gust,

Nathan tried not to think of the dangerous dry wash they'd crossed earlier that morning and the warning Mac had given about rushing water. He'd never look at a storm the same way again. Did the wash flood every time it rained? If it did, their situation had taken a serious turn for the worse. Mac had made it clear that the creek bed was uncrossable when flowing. They could be stuck here for days. They had a wedding to attend on Sunday, so if they didn't show up by Saturday evening Nathan was positive his partner, Jared, and best friend, Terry, would come looking for him. But the thought of staying out here in this predatory wilderness left him cringing.

Being totally out of his urban element—his comfort zone—the remote ruggedness of this land left Nathan more than a little ill at ease. He'd be the first to admit that he didn't have the skill set needed to survive in such a desolate place. After all, his idea of roughing it was a hotel with no room service. He wasn't cracked up for this nature stuff. The annual camping trips from his boyhood didn't offer any survival experience and provided no comfort.

His imagination ran amok as visions of being overcome by raging water flitted across his mind. Deep breathing exercises did nothing to calm his ratcheting nerves. Closing his eyes, Nathan said a prayer they wouldn't come across any treacherous flash flooding.

The temperature must have fallen at least twenty degrees in the last half an hour prompting an involuntary spasm of trembles. Nathan zipped up his coat, but the action did little to keep the brisk breeze from creeping through to his bones and rattling his teeth. Turning his focus to the horizon, he hoped to trick his mind into focusing on anything besides just how cold he was.

The farther they traveled into the desolate landscape, with a man they knew almost nothing about, sparked a sense of foreboding that had nothing to do with the weather. Had his face not been numb from the cold, he was sure he'd feel the worry lines as they grew deeper and etched his brow. Not only was the weather taking a turn for the worse his mind started playing tricks on him. They'd left civilization so far behind that this rugged land felt as though they'd been transported back in time—*way* back in time. His mind's eye imagined a covered wagon surrounded by hostile Indians. Hell, at this point, he wouldn't be surprised in the least if a pack of bloodthirsty warriors riding buckskin horses intercepted them. Not usually a man to entertain such wild imaginings, he silently chastised himself for the crazy daydreams. *Jeez! Get a grip!*

The mother of all headaches had been progressively building since they'd left the ranch house—probably due to the windshield. Nathan sneezed and then sneezed three more times in quick succession. Searching his coat pocket for a tissue, he cursed under his breath when he couldn't find one. "Dammit."

The dirt on this ranch was as fine as flour. So powdery, in fact, the dust billowed beneath the four-wheeler, behind the vehicle, to the side, and somehow even in front. The off-road vehicle had no doors or windows. Without a barrier to keep out the dust, the grimy particles covered Nathan and the other men with a layer of filth. His eyes burned, and his lungs wheezed as the dust continued its relentless attack on his senses—triggering a coughing fit. He feared clods of mud would dislodge from his lungs at any minute.

Even the discomfort of Nathan's headache and allergy issues did nothing to alleviate his growing apprehension. The barren landscape's vibe had each dust-coated hair on Nathan's body standing at attention. Feeling like a tightly wound spring ready at any given moment to pop loose, he focused on relaxing the taut muscles in his shoulders. For the moment, it was all he could do. *Don't panic. We'll all be out of here tonight.* He clung to that thought.

Clutching the roll bars to keep from being thrown from the vehicle, the men were jarred by yet another large rock that emerged in their path too fast to miss. The road, if you deigned to call it that, had all but disappeared a half hour ago. "I've got to ask"—Nathan scratched his head, trying to extricate some of the filth caught in his hair—"how do you know where we're going?" As far as he was concerned, they could've been traveling in circles. Everything looked the same.

Mac tapped the built-in compass on the dashboard. "The cabin is straight due north of the ranch house on a small mesa. When I flew over the property, I asked the helicopter pilot to give me coordinates of any outbuildings we located. I figured it was one less thing my men would have to do when they got here."

A man of few words, Mac went silent as he continued to concentrate on crossing the brutal terrain. Both Jursic and Nathan focused their attention on the countryside around them. This ranchland was a diverse ecosystem. Initially, they'd traveled for miles through pine trees. Sometimes thick. Sometimes sparse. Over the last five miles or so, gnarly cedars and piñon pine trees became the norm across the landscape. Small cactus plants dotted the land here and there. They'd canvassed every inch of the horizon for any sign of man or horse living or dead but came up empty.

Something dark and massive flashed in Nathan's peripheral vision. The unexpected movement had been jerky and unnatural. On impulse, his hand shot out and nudged Mac on the shoulder. "Stop!"

The four-wheeler skidded to a halt. Nathan leaped from the vehicle, trying his best to escape the dust cloud, and squinted to see as far into the trees as possible. His legs were restless. A moment ago, he'd been freezing. Now, his adrenaline kicked into high gear. He no longer felt the cold at all. "Did you guys see that?" Hoping the others didn't recognize the anxiety in the breathlessness of his voice, he cleared his throat.

The rumbling engine noise from the four-wheeler cut off. The men stepped up beside Nathan and peered into the distance. Mac scanned from tree to tree using a pair of binoculars. Jursic piped up, "What did you see?"

"I'm not sure. Whatever it was, it was quick." Nathan advanced another step when something crunched beneath his foot. Shifting his weight, he saw a small object sticking out of the micro-fine dirt. As he bent to pick it up, Mac finally answered his question. "I don't see anything with the binoculars. There's no movement anywhere."

Down on his haunches, Nathan looked up into the cowboy's face. "Do you find that strange? I'm just asking because whatever I just saw was the first moving object that I've seen out here. There haven't been any deer, rabbits, squirrels, birds, nothing. No sign of life whatsoever."

Mac tilted his cowboy hat up and scratched his forehead. "I'm a little surprised. This land should be great country for deer and antelope. It's a little low for elk and a little high for collared peccaries. Even so, I still would've expected to see at least one or two javelinas running around. They eat cactus pads and fruit. There's plenty of food for them here, but none of the plants have been touched."

Storing that little nugget of information in the back of his mind to think about later, Nathan's fingers combed through the dirt that felt more like baby powder. Unearthing the object that he'd stepped on he found a crude piece of hand-worked clay about the length and width of his little finger. He bent closer to further examine the item, and a shiver ran up his spine. *It can't be.* He'd stepped on a Native American artifact. The base was painted white, but there were intricate patterns drawn in black. On the tip of what looked to be a crude pipe was the head of an animal that seemed to have been fashioned by pinching the clay together while it was wet. The other men bent down and started combing through the dirt as well. They found other shards of pottery—some white with black markings, some painted brown with black markings.

"Look at this," Jursic exclaimed. Between his fingers, he held a perfectly intact arrowhead. "I've never seen a real arrowhead before."

Handing the tip of the pipe over to Mac, Nathan stood and started to pace around. Surveying the surrounding area, what he'd thought upon first glance had been small rocks and pebbles were actually pottery shards. They dotted the landscape everywhere he looked. What in the world had they stumbled upon? Was this place some kind of ancient Indian garbage dumping ground? He didn't think so. Although he didn't know much about historical Indian culture, he did know Native Americans took immense pride in the land and couldn't imagine them trashing it like this.

The wind whipped up sending another chill through Nathan. For the first time since leaving the ranch, he became still and took in the totality of the environment surrounding him. Something was off. Every instinct urged him to turn tail and get the hell out of here. He couldn't discern what the problem was, but his gut was screaming that there was danger all around them.

Nathan's gaze turned toward the area north of them, then south and back again. Closing his eyes, he focused on listening for any sound—no matter how small. Here they were out in the middle of nowhere, and it was dead silent.

How is it possible to drive deeper and deeper into territory that hadn't seen a human in God knows how long and not see or hear another living creature?

He'd grant that no animal sightings could be explained away easily enough. Most wild animals feared humans and became scarce as soon as someone entered the area around them. There being no deer could possibly be explained as the herd moving on to another area to feed, but as for the rest...At the very least birds should be calling their mates or singing. Grasshoppers should be chirping. Bees and other flying insects buzzing around. But there were no nature sounds at all.

And that's just plain crazy.

Nathan would swear on a stack of bibles that they were being closely observed. Moving his line of sight from the shadows to the treetops, he scanned the area for trail cams or any sign of human spying. There was nothing man-made visible. Still, his instincts were screaming that they'd been shadowed and relentlessly watched since departing the ranch house. The trouble with intuition was that there was no proof to back up the sensations. Until this point, he'd written off his feelings due to being in unfamiliar territory. But as they stood in the middle of nowhere amongst these small fragmented treasures from the past, he began to feel as though they were surrounded with no means of escape. Rubbing his scratchy, dirt filled eyes did nothing to calm his frayed nerves.

Before he could voice any concerns, Mac spoke up. "The cabin should be a couple of miles up the road. It shouldn't take us much longer to get there. I want to take a quick look at it and be back at the ranch before dark. So, we're going to have to step up the pace." Nathan nodded as he scrutinized the area. *Amen to that, brother.* The faster they got out of here, the better.

Using the binoculars to scan the terrain in the direction the four-wheeler was pointed, Mac continued, "It's easy enough to get around out here in the light of day—with a compass, but I'm not willing to chance what might happen when it gets dark. Let's get going while we still can."

Still ogling the arrowhead, Jursic sauntered toward the four-wheeler. "Wait," Nathan shouted a little louder than he'd intended. Both men turned and looked at him quizzically.

"I know this is going to sound odd, but I think we

need to leave the artifacts where we found them. At least for now." When their only response was blank stares, he continued, "I can't explain it, but it feels wrong, somehow, to remove them."

Mac held his hand out for Jursic to give him the arrowhead and a few pottery shards he'd collected. Moving quickly, he put each piece back. He turned and faced Nathan. "Good?"

Breathing a sigh of relief, Nathan nodded. "Good."

Chapter Six

As if their situation wasn't strange enough, while climbing back into the four-wheeler a dust devil appeared out of nowhere. While all three men shielded their faces from the blowing grime and grit, Nathan cursed the vehicle, before a silent plea crossed his lips that the fast-moving clouds didn't hold any rain.

Nathan couldn't help but scan the area around them once again. He knew down to his bones that they were being watched. Once seated, the tension he'd struggled with the last few hours outwardly presented itself as his foot nervously bounced in place.

We have to get out of here. Now.

As if he could read Nathan's mind, Mac's arm reached forward toward the ignition switch, but then froze. Glancing at their driver, Nathan noticed the creases near Mac's eyes growing deeper. His heart skipped a beat. "What's wrong?"

Shaking his head as if the action would provide clarity, Mac tapped the compass. "H-m-m. I've never seen that before."

Not liking the rancher's tone of voice, Nathan quickly inquired, "What?"

"Look at the compass."

Leaning over, Nathan watched as the needle spun wildly in circles. Jursic bumped him from behind to get a better view and sputtered, "What's it doing?"

Before the cowboy could answer, Nathan interrupted, "Are you sure it wasn't going crazy like that when we stopped?"

Mac continued to stare at their only means of navigation. "It was fine before I turned the vehicle off."

"What would make the needle spin like that?" There was a shrill timbre to Jursic's voice. *He's sensing danger too.* Nathan made a mental note to have a private discussion with his friend about losing his cool in front of clients when faced with uncomfortable situations. No matter what the circumstances, they represented Bastion Enterprises and needed to show a strong front. But he could certainly sympathize. This new sudden turn of events accelerated Nathan's stress to a whole new level. Given the urgency of their situation, it was becoming increasingly difficult to keep up a stoic pretense. Trying his best to get a grip, Nathan rubbed his temples. *How in the hell were they supposed to navigate this godforsaken land without a working compass?*

"I've used compasses to navigate my whole life. This is a new one on me." Mac looked to the sky and then out in front of the vehicle. Throwing his elbow over the seat, he glanced behind them. Both Nathan and Jursic followed suit.

The tracks directly behind them were visible, but they'd driven miles over solid rock. Given the lack of any marked road, he was confident their path wouldn't be discernible for much of their ride back. "What are your thoughts, Mac? Do you think we should take a pass on the cabin today and head back to the main house?" Nathan mentally crossed his fingers.

"We haven't got much sunlight left. If this storm weren't moving in, I'd say let's just continue on to the cabin. But without a compass, it may take us a little longer to find the place. Right now, we can follow our tire tracks back—at least for a while. If it rains or gets dark on us, we'll be out of luck. I think the safest thing to do would be to turn around and go back while we still can."

For the first time in hours, Nathan felt a sense of relief. The unnerving sensation of someone or something scrutinizing their every movement had gnawed at him all day. *Was it any wonder he was a ball of nerves?* He hadn't been able to shake the thought that they'd somehow been herded to this location out in the middle of bumfuck nowhere. If something were to attack, they'd be easy pickings. With a slight shake of the head to clear the crazy thoughts, Nathan kicked back in the seat and smiled for the first time in hours. With any luck, in no time at all, they'd be laughing over a good meal and a few imported beers. Preferably in the comfort of a nice little Mexican restaurant.

Jursic spoke up from the backseat. "Yeah. Let's get back."

Pivoting around to the steering wheel, Mac reached forward and turned the key. Nothing happened. Making another attempt, he switched the key off and on. The motor didn't sputter, didn't make a sound.

The unmistakable echo of his grinding teeth reverberated through Nathan's head. He had to restrain himself from slapping the rancher's hand away so he could have a go at starting the vehicle himself. This little backwoods jaunt was trying his fortitude. He swallowed what spit he had left. *Shit.*

Cursing under his breath, Mac jumped from the vehicle and lifted the hood. Nathan and Jursic both watched as he jiggled hoses and wires looking for any sign of the problem.

"That's just great!" The hood slammed down, and Mac turned to the men. "Nothing's loose. I don't see any obvious reason why it won't start."

Looking thoughtfully into the distance, he continued, "Well, boys, there's been a change in plans. It looks like we're going to have to hoof it to the cabin and ride the storm out there."

Their afternoon had just taken a nasty turn.

Jursic grabbed Mac's arm and spun him around. "What do you mean? We *can't* stay the night out here. We need to get back." Each word was elevated in pitch—reflecting his friend's alarm. Under ordinary circumstances, Nathan knew he should and would pull Jursic aside and talk him down from the ledge. But these were not normal circumstances. Not by a long shot.

Mac clenched his jaw. His steel gray eyes surveyed Jursic's frantic face and then Nathan's. "I'm sorry, but we've got to hurry. I don't like the idea of staying out here anymore than you do, but we'll be in even worse shape if we don't get to shelter soon." Looking up at the sky, he pursed his lips. "If we're lucky, we probably have about fifteen more minutes before we get soaked."

Moving quickly to the driver's side, the rancher bent over the seat and removed the .30-30 long gun and a box of ammo. Jursic was next to him in a millisecond. "Do you have another compass?"

Reaching into the backseat, Mac retrieved a gallon of water and a small duffle bag. Tossing the pack to

Jursic the rancher shook his head. "Nope. I've never needed an extra one before." The tough cowboy took a deep breath to compose himself before speaking again. It was obvious he wasn't used to explaining his every move. "Look. When you live your life on the land, you have to be prepared for anything. Trust me. You're in good hands. I might not know this property, but I've got thirty plus years of experience navigating through nature and surviving out in the elements. We've got shelter close by. This situation may seem bad, but it's no big deal.

"Now, we better get moving. Our only safe option is getting to the cabin, but we have to find it first." As if on cue, the air around them became electrified. In the time it would take to snap his fingers Nathan's lungs felt as if they had collapsed—losing every molecule of oxygen. Each hair on his body stood on end. A bolt of lightning flashed and struck a nearby tree. Time seemed to stand still. Jagged pieces of wood exploded and flew through the air, remedying the time warp. Starving for oxygen and scared, the men hit the ground just as a deafening thunderclap rang out.

Terrifying moments passed while they lay in a heap struggling to breathe. Mac finally yelled, "Is everyone okay?" The ringing in Nathan's ears muffled the rancher's voice as he continued, "That was too close for comfort. We have to get going. It's not safe out in the open!"

All three of the men scrambled to their feet. Mac's arm was stretched out and pointed at something ahead of them. "Look over there in the distance. From what I recall seeing during the flyover of the land, a copse of trees surrounded the line shack. The stand of pine was located about fifty yards north of a ridge. Do you see that mangled cedar at the crest of the ridge in front of us?"

"Yeah," Jurisc spoke up. "Do you remember seeing that tree?" The hope in his voice was unmistakable.

"Nope. There's no way I could identify a lone tree in this area." A quick shake of the head cemented Mac's answer and ramped up the stress level between the men. *We are so fucked,* Nathan thought.

"But I'm fairly certain the old cattle cabin is in the trees just beyond that point. The structure should be visible once we make the climb to that cedar." It was evident to Nathan that Mac's soothing tone of voice was meant to calm everyone. Surprisingly, it did. The man was a born leader. Under the circumstances, he had no problem following him. After all, what alternative did he have?

"While we walk, I'm going to teach you city boys how to navigate without a compass when you don't have the sun to guide you. Pay close attention. This information is important and could save your lives in the event we get split up."

Nathan's head jerked up. *Wait. What?* So much for feeling calm.

Understanding the importance of Mac's little speech, Nathan planned to focus on every word.

"We were heading straight north before the compass malfunctioned. See?" Mac pointed to the front of the four-wheeler. "To keep going in the right direction, you need to look as far as you can in the distance. Pick a landmark large enough that you'll have a constant visual on it as you walk. If you keep your eye on that big cedar, you won't venture too far off of your course.

"Once we get to that point, we should be able to locate the cabin. If we don't, then you turn around and line your sites up from the four-wheeler to the tree again. When you're sure you're lined up, turn around and you'll be facing straight due north again. Find another large identifying marker in the distance and start walking."

Mac glared at the men to make his point. His voice took on a stern edge. "Don't take cover in the trees. You saw what happened with that one. He tilted his head in the direction of the obliterated cedar. "Keep yourself low to the ground. You don't want to be the tallest thing around in a lightning storm either. You boys look like you're in shape, so I'm expecting you to keep up with me. Got it?"

"Got it," Nathan and Jursic answered in unison as they trotted behind Mac.

Chapter Seven

The line shack was exactly where Mac said it would be. Just as the cabin came into view, a loud rumble sounded in the distance behind them. They whipped around and saw a torrential wall of hail headed straight for them. The sky had indeed opened up, and hailstones the size of ping-pong balls came barreling along at a wicked pace.

Mac nudged them onward. "Quick! We don't want any part of that! Let's take cover inside."

There were no obvious signs of life as they converged on the covered front porch. If the missing men had been here, they were long gone now. As Nathan studied the line shack, it was hard to overlook all of the carelessly thrown together crosses. Just like the main ranch house, religious icons had been crudely fashioned with twigs, two by fours, tree branches— anything that could be tied or nailed together. Someone had taken the time to affix them to the outside walls of the small structure. *But why?* It was downright creepy. Who would go to all of this trouble when the cabin was meant to be used as a temporary shelter? Curiosity got the best of Nathan as he reached out and tugged on one. It didn't budge.

As he turned to discuss the bizarre use of crosses, Nathan noticed Mac kneeling just off of the covered porch studying the ground. Sporadic but heavy drops of rain preceded the hail and started pelting the area. Each massive drop hit the earth with such force that the dry powdered dirt kicked up in protest. Closing the distance between them, Nathan inquired, "What did you find? More pottery?"

Mac's gaze never wavered from the ground. "No. Quick! Take a look at this before the rain destroys everything. It doesn't make any sense."

Nathan bent down on his haunches just as Jursic uttered a low whistle and added, "Those must be some tough cowboys you have."

Mac shook his head forcefully in disbelief. "No! My cowboys would never step outside without their boots. Feet don't easily heal when you're on them all day. It's just not practical to be barefoot and risk the injury." His arm shot out and pointed to the side of the cabin. "It looks like there are hundreds of these human barefoot tracks that lead all around the cabin. I just don't..." Mac seemed to struggle for the appropriate remark and finally gave up trying. Straightening his tall body to its full height, he walked to the front door without saying another word.

Before the storm destroyed all of the newly found evidence, Nathan pulled his phone out to document the bizarre find by snapping pictures. Moving quickly around the cabin he'd realized that Mac had been correct. The footprints circled the small outbuilding in its entirety. He didn't have a clue as to what it meant, but it was another piece of the strange puzzle they were trying to put together.

Joining the men on the front porch, Nathan patted his clothing to shake off some of the dust. As the grime from the day billowed around them, he couldn't help but stare at the door. While the cabin seemed sturdy enough, the door looked like it belonged on Fort Knox. Five reinforced crudely fashioned cast iron hinges had been installed. Nathan wasn't sure if the windows ever had glass in them or not. Currently, they seemed to be boarded up from the inside. It didn't give him much hope for what they'd find when they finally entered the small shack.

Mac reached out for the doorknob, but Nathan grabbed his arm and stopped him. Peering back at the mysterious footprints, he whispered, "There may be someone inside." His line of vision moved higher and scanned the woods around them. "We're sitting ducks on this porch. We need to clear the cabin and get inside fast."

Without prompting Jursic pulled his weapon and swung his big body around toward the wilderness. Taking a knee to make himself as small as possible, he held the gun high and fanned it from side to side. Given the bizarre circumstances, he stated more calmly than Nathan would've thought possible, "I've got your backs. I'll wait to enter until I hear the all-clear."

Mac unzipped the duffle bag and pulled a flashlight out. "There's no electricity here. Since the windows are boarded up, it's going to be black as sin in there. Take this light. We'll need to breach fast." Raising his long gun, he continued, "I'm not sure of the layout. It's probably only one room. You go right and low. I'll go left and high."

Nathan nodded his assent.

Throwing the door open they made entry leaving Jursic to protect them from the rear. Thankfully the only thing that met them on the other side was shadows and musty air. Securing his weapon, Nathan yelled, "All clear, Jursic." His friend backed in through the entryway and shut the door behind him—only then did he reholster his gun.

Rummaging around the one-room cabin, they found a battery-powered lantern on the fireplace mantel. Once it was turned on it revealed a surprisingly tidy little space. To the left sat a long table that served as the kitchen area. They were lucky enough to find a propane camping stove, various canned goods, pots and pans, plastic wash basins, and four five-gallon jugs of water tucked beneath the table. Mac opened an airtight container to reveal paper plates, cups, and utensils. "All the comforts of home," the rancher quipped.

The rest of the cabin offered a sitting area complete with a fireplace and a full woodbin.

Inspecting the door, Nathan found five heavy-duty deadbolts spanning from top to bottom. There was also a two-by-four resting against the wall which when needed would settle into thick steel plates on either side of the door as a barricade.

No one was going to get through that. What in the world were these men trying to keep out? As suspected the windows had all been boarded up and nailed shut. And then there were the crosses—at least as many inside as out.

Circling their temporary quarters, Nathan nudged one of several large black plastic bags with his foot and found sleeping bags within. It appeared that the ranch hands had thought of everything when stocking this small space. He had to admit that under different circumstances and in a different location this wouldn't be too bad a place to spend some time. It was dry and secure and almost homey. But the weird vibe of the land and the insanity that must have sparked the implementation of so many crosses made Nathan's skin crawl.

Above them hail pelted their shelter with a horrendous clatter. The explosive sound was deafening inside the small line shack. They weren't going anywhere anytime soon. Making a fire and washing the dirt and grime off took priority over everything else.

Nathan kept an observant eye on Mac as he scrutinized one of the handmade crosses. He reached out but his hand abruptly halted just short of the crude crucifix. The cowboy's posture became stooped, and Nathan would swear the man's strong chin quivered. Retracting his arm, the rancher removed his hat. As if trying to get a grip on his emotions, he closed his eyes and ran his fingers through his hair. *H-m-m. Interesting.*

Regaining his composure, Mac remarked, "I'm relieved the men stocked the place before they left. We should be able to ride the storm out in relative comfort." The fact that the giant elephant in the room—the crosses—hadn't been mentioned surprised Nathan. Mac had shied away from that conversation altogether. Witnessing the rancher's emotional response the makeshift symbols evoked, he supposed it was possible that superstition lay behind the silence. *Maybe it's a cowboy thing.* Or who knows? Maybe the lack of conversation on the subject was nothing more than outright denial. Nathan had no clue. But one thing was certain—they were in for an extremely long evening. He'd let the odd reaction to the crosses drop for now. There'd be time later.

Advancing toward the door, Nathan slammed each of the deadbolts home and lifted the barrier in place. *Nothing's getting in here on my watch.*

"What did you do that for?" Jursic's voice rose in timbre with each word.

Nathan grinned just a bit at his friend's panicked tone. "I don't know about you, but if I enter a building and it's secured like a bank vault, I'm going to use every lock and blockade possible. I have no idea what the people before us were trying to keep out. So, to be on the safe side, we're locked in for the night. Since none of us are familiar with the terrain or what the potential dangers are, I don't think we should go outside by ourselves until daybreak. If one of us has to leave, we go together. Since we don't know what we're dealing with here, we're going to take all necessary precautions."

****

Feeling comfortable and a little more at ease now that he'd eaten, Nathan kicked back on the sleeping bag and gazed into the fire as it popped and danced. Being a large man, he rarely sat on the floor, but the lack of furniture left no other options.

The bone-deep chill had finally subsided. Nathan shut his eyes and breathed in the deep, rich scent of burning cedar. The tangy, woodsy smell soothed his tired soul. This moment was the first chance he'd had to unwind since waking up this morning. Come hell or high water he was going to enjoy it while he could.

Jursic, grumbling under his breath, captured Nathan's attention. The man paced from corner to corner of the small space holding the phone above his head to check for service. It was apparent that he was wrestling with a severe case of the heebie geebies. At this pace, he'd never relax enough to find his Zen moment. He allowed that thought to settle and smiled. *As if Jursic would even know what a Zen moment was.*

Nathan had learned long ago that one of life's biggest lessons was to grab downtime when you could and get as much yardage from it as possible. Considering the bizarre circumstances they were facing, there was bound to be another dust-up sooner or later. Unless you wanted to end up with ulcers, you couldn't worry about whatever problem you were facing every second.

Glancing over at Mac, who was quietly gazing into the fire, he couldn't help but notice how much the man had loosened up. The deep worry lines he'd sported earlier were nonexistent now. He seemed almost peaceful.

The hail had long since disappeared along with the loud banging it produced on the rooftop. The rain, however, had fallen steadily for the last two hours. The slight patter was enough to provide a mesmerizing sense of peace and calm.

"I miss this," Mac uttered to no one in particular as he stared into the flames. "The business end of running the ranch takes too much of my time. I hate computers and accounting, but they're a necessary evil."

Now was as good a time as any to see if Mac would open up about his personal life. He needed somewhere to start his search for enemies. "Are you married, Mac?"

His face tightened up, and he momentarily shut his eyes. "I was."

Nathan mulled over Mac's answer. Maybe an ex-wife had something to gain by sabotaging the Arizona branch of the Aces and Eights. "When did you get divorced?"

This time the rancher's face lost all its color. "My wife died last year during childbirth. The baby died too." The words, no more than a whisper, conveyed undisguised vulnerability and pain. Two characteristics he never would have associated with the big man.

A full-blown lump of compassion developed in Nathan's throat making it difficult to speak. "I'm so sorry for your loss."

As if to repel the sympathy, Mac's hand waved Nathan's words off. "It's my fault she died. My wife, Rose, was a frail woman. Truth be told, she didn't like being stuck out in the middle of nowhere. Living on a ranch is a hard life and not meant for everyone.

"Rose wasn't due for another two weeks. It was our first child, and the doctor assured us we had plenty of time." After an agonizingly long pause, Mac continued, "We had a record snowfall in January of last year. Every man on the ranch, including myself, had to work twenty-four hours a day to save the herd. I have some large structures set up near the house for protection from the weather. Me and my men had to go out into the blizzard and round up as many head of cattle that we could find. For those that couldn't be located, we left bales of hay so they could at least eat.

"The weather was so bad that we couldn't even use the four-wheelers. The only way around was on horseback. Even that mode of transportation was sketchy. I came home one morning just before the sun came up. I turned the coffee on and went upstairs to check on Rose. She was dead. She'd gone into labor while I was out on the range. The baby was breech." There was a slight hitch in his voice as he spoke of the traumatic moment. Mac rubbed his face, but the action did nothing to relieve the anguish Nathan witnessed on the man's features.

Jursic had stilled as Mac conveyed his story. It wasn't long before he gave up the frantic search for a signal and joined them on the floor. Ever the funny man, his partner fussed and fought with a sleeping bag and finally just threw it in a heap next to Mac. Nathan recognized this move for what it was. Jursic, a good man, planned to introduce a little levity to lighten the mood. In that respect, the big guy reminded him a lot of his best friend, Terry. Neither one of these men could stand by and watch someone hurting. Their unique sense of humor always came through and improved everyone's spirits. He couldn't wait to hear what Jursic would say or do to soothe this man's pain.

Several minutes of silence passed as they listened to the patter of the rain. Jursic chimed in, "I'm currently dating a witch. I could hook you up if you're interested." The absurd comment did what it was intended. They all laughed.

Curious, Nathan asked, "Which witch?" He bumped Jursic's knee. "You see what I did there?"

Coming out of his stupor, Mac snickered. "Exactly how many witches do you know?" Nathan was sure Mac thought Jursic was teasing him.

"A whole coven, brother." Turning to Nathan, Jursic beamed. "I took Cheryl out last weekend. It was our first date, but we're going to see each other again."

Mac sat up. "Are you serious? You're actually dating a *witch*—a real-life witch?"

Jursic beamed. "That would be correct."

"When you say witch—are we talking *The Good Witch* or something more along the lines of *Into the Woods?*"

Grinning from ear to ear, Jursic replied, "I'm impressed! For living out in the middle of no-where-ville, Montana, you, sir, know your filmography. My little witch is all girl, sugar and spice and everything nice. There's not a wicked bone in her body."

Nathan laughed at the description and had to add his two cents. "If I were you, I'd be careful, Jursic. I don't know how kindly Cheryl would take it if she heard you describing her as an innocent little girl. I might just have to tell her." Shifting his gaze back to the rancher, Nathan patted his chest over his heart. "I'll tell you, Mac, that little witch is pure siren.

"You might as well start preparing yourself now to meet some of the—dare I say—strangest and captivating people. I'd trust every one of them with my life—and have on more than one occasion. Since there's no way in hell we're going to leave you out here by yourself, you're going to join us for the wedding of the century.

"I grew up with a girl named Jody. Her specialty is speaking to the dead." The mere thought of the woman produced a grin from ear to ear. "If I had to describe her skills, I'd say she's a spirit psychologist. They always seem to seek her out for help.

"My best friend, Terry, is marrying Rainy on Sunday. She's the High Priestess of the Circle of the Pines Coven and possibly the most badass woman I've ever met in my life."

"No shit?"

"Nope. And Cheryl, the woman Jursic did such a poor job describing, is her assistant." Turning back to his friend, Nathan added, "Are wedding bells in your future too? Everyone seems to be getting married these days."

Jursic blanched and made a production of tossing his hands in the air. "Nah. We like spending time together, but we're more on the friend scale than anything else. She's a lot of fun, but the *I-can't-keep-my-hands-off-of-you* chemistry really isn't there for either of us."

Nathan's partner purposely turned toward the rancher and smiled. "By the way, Mac, Nathan's in love with a Native American Princess."

Nathan froze. *Now, the man had gone too far.* "Careful." The menacing tone of his voice should have been warning enough, but Jursic was never the sharpest tack in the box. Stretching his leg out so he could tap Mac's foot, his partner persisted with sharing too much information. "Get a load of this. The big guy, here, is too afraid to talk to her." Jursic slapped his knee and cackled.

"Wait just a damn minute. You don't know—" Mac's raucous laughter rang out, stymieing Nathan's response.

Jursic offered an apologetic grin while tipping his head toward the rancher. His dignity had just been sacrificed so a man they'd met today would feel better. Nathan shot Jursic his best *you're-dead-when-I-get-you-alone* glare. Once the cowboy's laughter died down, he stated with a big shit-eating grin, "Is that so? I didn't take you for being scared of much."

Great. Now everyone was on his damn case.

"I'm *not* afraid to talk to her. You're not getting the whole story. I've only met her once." *But I dream about her every night.* Somehow that fleeting thought made him angrier.

"Pfft. If you're not going to be honest with yourself, I can't do a thing to help you," Jursic added as he passed his phone to Mac. "Here, check this picture out."

Mac glanced at the phone. What appeared to be appreciation sent his eyebrows into his hairline. With a big toothy grin, the man whistled. "She's beautiful, Nathan. Why don't you want to talk to her?"

Perplexed, Nathan could only offer up a blank stare. Leaning forward he grumbled, "Let me see that phone."

Upon viewing the photo, Nathan's whole body froze. Bright Flower's glowing face shone back at him in the form of a sketch. He recognized the drawing as Terry's work immediately. Without thinking, he touched the screen to magnify the picture. His heartbeat started to race, and everyone in the room was a distant memory.

The fact that Jursic had Bright Flower's likeness on his phone struck him like a ton of bricks. *Is this so-called friend trying to move in on my territory?* Nathan glared at Jursic. "Why would Terry let you take a picture of this? You haven't even met her." Nathan's stomach tightened at the thought. *"Have* you?"

Jursic opened his mouth, but before he could explain Nathan threw the phone back at him and growled. "You leave her alone. She's special and deserves better than any of us."

"Look, Nathan, Terry's concerned, and frankly

after witnessing this little outburst I can see why. He's your best friend. I didn't believe him when he told me the story behind Bright Flower. Both he and Rainy asked me to discuss this with you when the opportunity presented itself. They said you wouldn't listen to them and that maybe I could talk some sense into you before it's too late and you lose her for good." Jursic scooted closer.

As soon as I get out of this place, I'm going to kick Terry's ass.

Nathan's rage got the better of him. He'd zoned out for a moment picturing the many ways he would torture Terry. As his conscious became present again, Jursic was conveying the whole sordid situation to Mac. "That's right, Mac. I can't believe it's still done. Spirit Keeper, Bright Flower's grandfather, is looking to make an arranged marriage for her. From what I understand she's quite a catch in the Navajo community. Men are flocking to ask for her. There's one in particular that the grandfather is leaning toward."

Nathan jumped to his feet. His heart pounded so hard that he slid a hand to his chest for relief. Panic captured his body in an icy grip. Every muscle was affected, and his knees weakened to the point they barely held him upright. "*What?* How would you know that?"

"I'm friends with Terry too, remember? *He's* the one who told me. Since Rainy is in constant communication with Bright Flower and Spirit Keeper, she stays up to date on the whole marriage thing. If you ask me, she's doing that so if the need arises, she can intercede on your behalf since you're too much of a chicken shit to do it yourself."

Nathan's knees threatened to buckle. Before he fell, he took a seat on the floor.

Jursic inched closer. "Nathan, your feelings are written all over your face. You've got to go and talk to Spirit Keeper before he accepts someone else's offer of marriage. Stall him. Do whatever you need to for the process to slow down."

Pissed now for airing too much personal information in front of a stranger—a client no less—Nathan growled out, "Shove it, Jursic. I mean it. This subject is not open for debate."

"Excuse me," Mac butted in. "This is none of my business, but I'm going to offer my two cents anyway. If there is even a remote chance that this is the *woman* you're meant to spend the rest of your life with, you've got to do something. Don't let your feelings of inadequacy steer you in the wrong direction."

Nathan rubbed his eyes—wishing this conversation would end. It was torture. He opened his mouth to cut it short, but Mac held his hand out to stop him.

"Think about it this way, Nathan. I don't know your friend Terry or his bride Rainy. But if you were to ask Terry if he believed he was good enough for Rainy, what do you think the answer would be? H-m-m? Do you believe for a minute that there is a man alive that ever thinks he is deserving of the woman he loves?" That got Nathan's attention. He glared at the cowboy. It was well past time that he minded his own business.

As they stared at one another, Mac broke the visual contact first with a dip of his head. Nathan was sure the man was giving him time to digest the little nugget of wisdom he'd offered by throwing another log on the fire. Pivoting his big body, Mac faced him and grunted.

For just a moment, he'd withdrawn his walls and allowed his heartache—the likes of which Nathan couldn't imagine—shroud his features. "Take it from me. Time's too short to waste. If you really do have feelings for the Indian Princess, you've got to make your move. Tomorrow may never come."

Nathan's mouth went dry. He wiped his lips with the back of his hand.

Jursic—obviously proud of himself—beamed while tossing a pack of cards on the floor between them. "While our love lives are an interesting topic, it's depressing as hell. How about we liven things up? I found these. Let's play some poker to pass the time." He pulled his wallet out and riffled through the bills. "I've got one hundred and fifty bucks to pony up."

After the humiliation he'd just suffered, Nathan couldn't wait to take every damn dime Jursic had. "You're on."

It only took an hour to relieve Jursic of his wad. Nathan yawned and stretched his arms over his head. "Let's turn in. We've got a long walk ahead of us tomorrow. I want to get started as soon as the sun comes up."

It felt like forever before the events of the day finally wound down sufficiently for Nathan's mind to relax enough to sleep. As usual, his last thought was of Bright Flower.

Chapter Eight

This dream was truly vivid. It was as if the slumber he'd fallen into had turned into a separate, but extremely real world...

The massive bison lumbered along the moonlit path at a leisurely pace. The beast had somehow become a part of Nathan since he'd started dreaming of his beautiful Indian princess. The animal was never far from his side.

Straddling the buffalo, Nathan held Bright Flower snug against his bare chest. Her long tresses drifted with the light breeze, gently stroking his arms and shoulders—sparking shivers of pleasure. The warmth of her generous curves—a direct contrast to his solid male build—tormented him with a scorching carnal need. But she was untouched. He respected her far too much to cross that line even in his dreams. But, oh, how he longed to caress her and teach her the ways of a man and woman.

The eagle that always accompanied Bright Flower in his dreams nestled into the buffalo's mane and nuzzled the beast's enormous head with its sizeable hooked beak. Chuffing his approval, the bison, rocked its head, first right and then left to give the raptor better access.

Bright Flower tilted her head and placed a soft kiss

on the underside of Nathan's jaw. "My eagle loves your buffalo as much as I love you. She can't wait for me to go to sleep so we can visit you. When are you going to ask for me so we can end this torture?" Knowing full well that this conversation was purely wishful thinking, he couldn't help but indulge in the fantasy.

Squeezing Bright Flower tighter, Nathan rubbed his cheek on the crown of her head. The clean woodsy scent of her hair ignited a fire deep in his soul. This quiet contentment was what he sought night after night in his make-believe dream world. If only he could find this gratification in his waking world. Life would be complete with Bright Flower by his side. Knowing their time together was short, Nathan set aside all the distractions that reality held and consciously made an effort to throw himself deeper into the dream.

A brilliant shooting star dazzled the dark evening sky. Nathan pointed to show Bright Flower, but she quickly jerked his hand back and cradled it to her chest as she blew a puff of breath skyward.

"What are you doing?"

"Quickly, blow at the star!"

Bright Flower's superstitious nature inspired a huge grin. He never wanted to do anything that made her unhappy, so he puckered up and blew at the fading tail of the meteor. Nathan enjoyed learning the traditional Navajo Way of things even if some of the practices seemed a bit over the top on the foolish scale. And it seemed this one was a bit strange also. But after all, who was he to step on other people's beliefs?

Holding his hand up, she squeezed his index finger. "In our culture, you should never point with your finger. And you should not stare at shooting stars."

"So, let me get this straight. No looking at falling stars, and no pointing with any finger." How in the world did her people keep all of these rules straight? "Got it. But what do you do if you want to direct someone's attention to something?"

Twisting her upper body so he could see her better, his Indian goddess puckered her mouth. Nathan happily obliged the request and bent to kiss her full ripe lips. Bright Flower's soft coo nearly sent him over the edge of reason. He tortured himself further by deepening the kiss.

"M-m-m. That was nice, Nathan, but not what I meant." She playfully flicked his nose. "Pay attention. If you want to point something out to someone, you pucker your lips toward the object. Or you can tilt your head and point with your nose. Like this." She demonstrated, and he became even more enamored. She was so damn beautiful.

The thought of him puckering up at another man instead of pointing prompted a chuckle. "Okay. But I prefer my meaning of puckered lips over yours. So— not to be obnoxious or anything—but why don't you point with your finger? It's so much easier."

She giggled and stroked his cheek. "Watch and then you tell me." It was apparent that Bright Flower loved the role of teacher. Her face transformed as she sneered and squinted. She was trying to project anger, but she'd seriously missed the mark. This mysterious woman whom he adored beyond measure was no actress. He had to focus on keeping his features flat to refrain from smiling. Her arm flew out and pointed to the trees. She kept grunting and jabbing at the air as if it annoyed her. Once she'd completed her little demonstration, her face brightened with a broad smile. "So? Now do you understand why you don't point with your finger?"

Nathan scratched his chin and offered an o-o-h and a-h-h while pretending to concentrate. Finally, he just shook his head and grinned. "I got nothin'. Sorry."

Bright Flower playfully jabbed him in the solar plexus. After a dramatic sigh, she continued her schooling. "Nathan, pointing your finger is a sign of aggression. It could be forgiven if you point with urgency to a threat in the distance, such as a fire or a dangerous animal, but you must never, never point at another person. Doing so would be misunderstood and could get you into a lot of trouble."

"Okay. I understand. No pointing. Teach me something else. What other taboos should I know about?"

Accepting the challenge Bright Flower's gaze journeyed across the scenery while contemplating the next lesson. After a moment she charmed him with a grin. "Look." Her head bobbed as she pointed with her nose. "Do you see that tree? It's broken and scorched."

Searching the moonlit horizon Nathan nodded when he spotted the burnt, splintered remains of a large cedar tree. "Yes. Wait..." His body shuddered causing his legs to constrict. The spirit animal beneath him was highly attuned to his thoughts. The buffalo snorted and stumbled to a halt. "I was standing about twenty-five yards away from that tree when it was hit by lightning today." Trying to get his bearings, he scanned the horizon for the four-wheeler which should've been parked in the area. It wasn't there.

Nathan internally chided himself. Of course, it isn't

there. I'm dreaming. There's no way in hell I'd allow Bright Flower anywhere near this godforsaken land.

The buffalo must have sensed his calming mind and swung its huge head looking for guidance. Nathan pressed his heels into the animal's side, and the beast complied with a slow gait.

The beautiful woman in his arms beamed. "Nathan, I'm not sure where this place is, but that tree is special. It holds great power for you. I must consult with grandfather on this matter." Unable to understand the intensity edging her words, he was pleased when she relaxed, and serenity once again crossed her features. "I don't know what it means yet, but you are an extraordinary man, my Nathan, to garner such a gift from the Creator.

"Now, let's continue your lessons. When you come upon a tree or rock that has been struck by lightning, you must never touch them. The scorched remains of such items are considered sacred and should be handled only by singers."

"Singers?"

"You would call us shamans or medicine men, or women in my case. In my culture, we are called singers because we chant to call on the Creator for healing and other reasons. This is a serious matter. You must take heed. When you happen across partially burnt wood, take a wide path. If lightning had indeed struck the blackened timber, and you handle the wood which was felled by the Creator, you will become ill or have bad luck. The scorched lumber was touched and felled by the Holy One, and therefore must be handled with reverence."

"I've got a lot to learn."

"Does that bother you?"

Nathan squeezed her again. "Not if you're my teacher." The buffalo stumbled, catching Nathan and Bright Flower off guard. They barely kept their seats. The beast grunted and gyrated, shifting its weight. The enormous head swung back and forth while chuffing and spewing thick threads of saliva in all directions. Muscles rippled beneath their legs as the bison twisted and pivoted in circles. The warning signs were unmistakable. Danger was close at hand. Bright Flower's eagle flapped its wings and took to the sky screeching an alert.

"What's happening?" Bright Flower cried. Clutching his woman to keep her from being thrown, Nathan grabbed a fistful of the beast's hair but struggled to stay perched on the animal's back.

One final stumble and Bright Flower was wrenched from Nathan's hold. Shrieking she lurched forward and hung onto the bison's mane for dear life. The mighty beast's hooves would crush her if she fell. Replacing the serenity of dream play was an ominous fear that was all too real. A swift spiraling dust devil came out of nowhere and snatched Bright Flower from the grip of his dream. Her terrified screams tore through the night air as she disappeared into the sky.

The buffalo pitched forward once more and lost its footing. Unable to maintain his grip, Nathan was thrown from the bison's back. Swiftly regaining his feet, he kept the beast behind him to protect his flank and prepared himself for an attack. The air around him became dense as another deep guttural grunt from the bison sounded a warning to all who threatened.

Wake up! I need to wake up! I'm dreaming. That's

all this is—just a dream. Nothing can hurt me here. Wake up!

The words rolled on a loop through his brain, but he remained trapped in this nightmare.

A sleek mountain lion emerged out of the blackness and invaded their space. Raised hackles spiked the length of the cat's back. The creature bared its teeth which appeared to be as sharp as ice picks. This new danger sent Nathan into a defensive crouch. He cringed and ducked his head as the cat leaped into the air landing soundlessly in front of him. The puma's head jerked around—its gaze locked on whatever unseen danger the inky darkness hid. As the cat unleashed a blood-curdling yawl, Nathan realized the animal wasn't there to do him harm. Like a guardian angel, the mountain lion was protecting him just as the buffalo was trying to do.

Somewhere off in the distance, the sound of Indians chanting could be heard. His blood all but froze. "What the fuck?" With each second that passed, the terrifying voices grew in intensity. The warbling yells were so close now, that Nathan felt he could reach out and touch the aggressors. But they remained unseen. There must be hundreds of people surrounding him.

The chaotic moment suddenly stilled. The quiet was almost worse than the terrifying screeches. Nathan's heart pounded so hard he was aware of every beat. It was the only sound that broke the petrifying silence. Securely gripped in terror's clutches, his chest tightened and refused to expand for a single life-giving breath.

A coyote yipped in the distance. Then another. And

another. The petrifying chorus of wild carnivores surrounded Nathan. What had happened to all of the Indians? How had they escaped?

He was going to die. Even though he was dreaming, Nathan knew this was the end. Bright Flower's face flashed in front of his eyes and sorrow over missed opportunities replaced the terror. His life would be extinguished without him ever knowing the taste of her lips or the feeling of cradling her in his embrace while being awake. All he had were dreams.

Sandwiched between the cougar and bison, Nathan had all but given up. Lightning cut through the air, and a sharp clap of thunder cracked above his head. Spirit Keeper, Bright Flower's grandfather, dropped from the sky. With a crude bow pointed into the blackness the man flung an arrow at an invisible target. Riveted Nathan watched the projectile slice through the black night—leaving a contrail of bright white light just as the meteor had earlier. Judging by the distant sound of a coyote's distressed yelp Nathan imagined the arrow had hit its mark.

While looking far into the distance, the old man's free hand found the cat's forehead and ran his fingers from ear to ear. Throwing his head back, Spirit Keeper released a mighty war cry, the mountain lion accompanying him with one of his own. Pivoting, Bright Flower's grandfather pushed Nathan into the bison's side with the force of a much younger, stronger man. "You must wake now. You're in danger! Don't open the door until the sun rises! Do not open the door! I'll bring help."

Nathan woke from the dream covered in sweat. Lying there with his eyes open, he tried to orient himself by breathing deeply. Listening to the predawn sounds, he realized the rain had all but stopped. All that was left was a surprisingly calming plinking noise as the pitched roof evacuated itself of the remaining moisture. *Plop. Plop. Plop.* The sound so soothing, he focused on each drop to slow his mind enough to score another half an hour of shut eye.

On the edge of sleep, another more unsettling noise caught his attention. Instantly alert, Nathan sat up to try and discern what exactly he was hearing. An animal scratching at the door? *A raccoon maybe?* While Nathan found it strange that a wild animal would want to be anywhere near a human, he was more than a little relieved to discover that there was life on this desolate land.

Rolling over, he tucked his arm under his head. Just as he got comfortable a blast of static filled the quiet as all three walkie talkies roared to life. Nathan's heart almost stopped as the white noise rapidly built in decibels. In the time that it took to hop to his feet, the racket was so loud that he was afraid his eardrums might burst. Covering his ears, he wasn't surprised that the other two men were up and frantically searching for the reason behind the screeching noise.

Just as fast as the audible assault began, everything went quiet again—although the vibrations of the traumatic grating noise still rang loudly in his inner ear. It was as though someone had thrown a switch. The three men stared at each other. Just outside of the wooden walls, Nathan heard the distinct sound of someone or something circling the cabin and sloshing through the mud. Whatever or whoever was making that noise, there were too many to count. Nathan's heart sank as he remembered the ominous dream which now seemed more prophetic than not. A wild pack of coyotes came to the forefront of his mind. Mac had told them earlier to expect a late-night visitation from the carnivores. The scavengers were known to follow people and steal any food left behind. They'd surely smelled them. That had to be what was happening.

Feeling a little better about the situation Nathan took a deep breath to calm his overactive imagination. *No harm done.* The intruders were simply animals doing what came naturally. They were outside, and the men were barricaded safely inside. The scavengers would move on once they figured out there was nothing here for them to eat.

A booming crash hit the roof of the cabin as if something huge had fallen out of the sky. The men hit the floor and scurried to the center of the room, forming a small circle back to back. A wicked screech—an unearthly mixture of a deep, guttural growl and the whistle of a bird of prey—sent waves of fear through Nathan's body, jostling his nerves to the near breaking point. The men readied their weapons—against what they had no clue.

"What the fuck was that?" Mac yelled.

The door shook and rattled then stopped. Every weapon quickly turned toward the entryway. Heavy footsteps cruised across the roof, each followed by a strange scratching noise as if the feet or paws of whatever it was sported sharp claws.

A lone coyote wailed behind the cabin. Another joined in. And then another. And just like the dream, it wasn't long before the haunting call turned into wild excited yips that surrounded the one-room building.

The banging footfalls on the roof grew louder and more frenzied. Whatever was up there was no damn coyote. The creature didn't shuffle and scurry as if running around on all fours. There was no grace to the movement. Each thud of the gait shook the tiny cabin and threatened to break the building apart. Dust particles rained down from the weight of the creature's frenzied prancing, and Nathan prayed the ancient ceiling would hold. Another terrifying shriek sounded from above as if the devil himself were throwing a wicked tantrum.

The wild dogs scratched on every wall of the cabin trying to gain entry. Some barked. Some howled. And some had a terrifying warble to their voices that sounded more human than animal. Loud bangs echoed off of every exterior wall. The dogs must be running full speed at the line shack and throwing their bodies against the barrier.

Suddenly, everything stopped. The men were granted a few blessed moments of silence. Nathan as well as the other two had barely started to regain their wits when a screeching high-pitched whistle, combined with a baying shriek bellowed from just above their heads again. The predator responsible for that eerie sound seemed to be controlling the wild animals surrounding the cabin. Whatever caused that god-awful noise wasn't human or animal. Nothing made any sense. The shrill call sent the coyotes surrounding the cabin into a frenzy. Their bodies furiously rammed the walls, yelping in pain and disappointment as their efforts to gain entry continued to fail. Mac threw more wood onto the fire to up the blaze and to cut off any possible means of access from the chimney.

"What the hell kind of an animal made that noise?" Nathan finally yelled.

Pointing the rifle to the ceiling, Mac responded, "I've never heard anything like that before. Whatever that thing is, it's working them up into a frenzy."

Another earsplitting shriek from above and instantaneously everything went silent. *Had the animals left to chase other prey?* Not knowing what to make of this Nathan cleared his throat but the action did little to tamp down the agonizing terror.

Mac tilted his head, as if the action allowed him to hear better. His brow furrowed while raising his fingers to his lips. "Listen. Do you hear that?"

Straining his senses to the limit proved fruitless. Nathan couldn't hear a thing. He didn't believe, however, that any noise could be more horrifying than whatever had landed on the roof. He tiptoed across the room and placed his ear against the door. He was wrong. There *was* something scarier.

Just like in the nightmare, low guttural chanting caught Nathan's attention. He didn't want to think about the dream, though, because in the end, he hadn't been able to save himself. Spirit Keeper had come to his rescue. These bizarre events couldn't be real. Maybe, if he was lucky, this was another dream. He pinched himself as hard as he could. *Dammit! This is no nightmare.*

The petrifying Native American cries grew in pitch and fervor. Unable to reconcile whatever this predicament was, Nathan took a full step away from the door. His muscles so tense, they vibrated. When the anxiety peaked at its highest, Nathan yelled, "This is fucking crazy! We're not in the nineteenth century.

What the hell is going on here? It sounds like a whole tribe of Indians wailing war cries and closing the distance between them and us by the second. How can—"

A loud whooshing noise sounded from above. The fire's flames fanned out, and smoke billowed into the room. *Oh God! Whatever that thing is, it's smart enough to smoke us out.* The men choked and coughed. Another whoosh and the creature on the roof must have lifted off and taken flight. The sickening sound of talons scratching the surface as it paraded back and forth had ceased.

Before they could relax, two massive strikes hit the roof and sent the men within the cabin scattering to different corners. Nathan could only pray that the top of the building was as fortified as the walls had proven to be. All weapons were pointed upward. A menacing growl sounded, soft at first but grew in intensity. The angry yowl of the mountain lion from Nathan's dream boomed and silenced all other predators—animal and human alike. A second roaring howl, this time human, joined the first. Somehow, just as in the nightmare, Spirit Keeper and his feline companion had made an appearance for the sole purpose of protecting them. *But how is that possible? I'm not dreaming.*

It was senseless to waste time trying to understand Spirit Keeper's presence. Nathan's knees buckled from relief and sent him staggering across the floor with arms raised. "I know this sounds crazy, but we're safe now."

Mac and Jursic both gaped at him. There was a crazed look in Jursic's eyes as he pointed his weapon toward the ceiling. "No!" Nathan leaped on his friend and knocked the gun to the floor. "It's Spirit Keeper. He's protecting us. Listen! The voices and animal calls are almost gone. That thing that was on our roof has run away."

Nathan envisioned the magical puma stalking from one side of the roof to the other as the animal roared again. Spirit Keeper's voice boomed into the fireplace. "Do not come outside until it is light. There is danger all around. In one hour, leave this place. When the time comes, run. Your lives depend on it. Keep to the meadows in the open and stay clear of the trees and shadows. By the time you reach your vehicle, Spirit Talker's man should've arrived to get you to safety." They waited anxiously for another five minutes, but there was only silence. Mac pivoted to Nathan and asked, "Who the hell is Spirit Talker?"

Relieved beyond measure, Nathan shrugged. "I have no idea. I guess we'll find out soon enough."

Chapter Nine

Mac tapped his watch and said, "It's been an hour. It's time to get the hell out of here."

As Nathan unbolted the locks, he stated, "I'll go first. Mac, you're in the middle. Jursic will take up the rear." He glanced over his shoulder. "Is everyone ready?" Both men nodded, and Nathan jerked the door open.

As instructed the men bolted from the tree covered area where the line shack was located. Panic and the resolve to escape with their hides intact overrode every emotion and drove them forward. They didn't even take the time to canvas the surroundings for clues as to what had attacked them last night. There'd be time for that later when reinforcements arrived.

The previous night's storm had taken a toll on the land. Surprisingly, there wasn't any running or standing water, but the powdery dirt had received a soaking and turned to a spongy clay slop—slowing their race to safety. With each footfall, their feet slid and sank at least six inches into the sludge. Layer upon layer of the unforgiving mud adhered to their feet and legs.

Nathan made the mistake of stopping to check the progress of the men behind him. He didn't want to lose contact with either of them. God only knew what would happen if they were separated. Satisfied they were close he willed his legs to move, but nothing happened. He was stuck. The ground was swallowing him whole. Throwing his back into the task, he yanked one leg free and came up shoeless. "Dammit!" Even though his hikers were secured with double knots, the earth had gobbled them up and refused to give them back. With Spirit Keeper's warning of danger in the trees and shadows fresh in his mind, he wrote his shoes off as another casualty of this bizarre outing. "Barefoot it is. I can do this." He pulled the other leg free.

Each step closer to safety became more difficult as the muck clung to their clothing. Nathan couldn't escape the feeling that some force of nature was doing its level best to trap them on this miserable land. His imagination insisted on running wild and would be his undoing if he couldn't get these ridiculous thoughts under control.

What the hell was going on here? They were currently in a fight for their lives against the terrain. But beyond that...*what?* Hostile Indians? A pack of hungry coyotes? Maybe ghosts of the past? Or were they all just figments created by group hysteria? The terrifying events had certainly seemed real enough early this morning. The only action keeping panic at bay was one deep breath after another. Every movement closer to freedom was a hellacious struggle. Not being the type of person to scare easily, Nathan recognized that he was riding on the edge of a paranoid precipice. If he couldn't find a way to hightail his ass off quickly, whatever nerve he had left would be lost.

Rubbing his brow, Nathan bit his lip to feel the sting in hopes of holding onto his sanity. He grunted, clenched his teeth, tightly grasped his jeans at the waist to keep them up, and trudged on. *I don't know what or who you are, but you're not going to fucking beat me!*

Nathan was so relieved to see the big cedar marking the top of the ridge that he bent at the waist and grabbed his knees. He felt like he'd won a marathon. Peering over his shoulder, he couldn't contain his grin. "We made it, boys. The safety of the clearing is just below us."

Spirit Keeper had promised to call for help, but Nathan had no idea how that help would materialize. Hell, at this point, he wouldn't be surprised to see the old man swoop down on them riding a pet dragon. Bright Flower's ancient granddaddy had a lot of explaining to do. For now, though, they were still on their own and hell-bent on getting out of the area.

Given the poor conditions moving at a fast clip was not an option. If they wanted to make it down the ridge to the abandoned four-wheeler in one piece, they'd have to tread carefully on the downhill path. With no trees to protect the slope from the rain, the mud-laden trail leading to safety was even deeper and slicker.

While cautiously navigating through the treacherous slop, Nathan's foot squished and slid through the muck. A sharp jab to the sensitive skin on his arch caused him to yelp. Fighting to pull his foot free, he started to slip and threw his arms out, pinwheeling them to stop the momentum. "Whoa!" It took a monumental effort to keep his balance in the slime. *Nothing's easy out here.*

Not wanting to cause any further damage to his already sore feet, he kept his lower body stationary and pivoted his torso to glance back at Mac, and then Jursic who was positioned at the rear. "We're going to have to take it slow, at least until we get to the bottom. This mud is dangerous and hiding all sorts of sharp things.

"Try to find a stick to…" Before he could finish the thought, Jursic's big body jerked forward. His arms waved in the air but did nothing to help regain his balance. His friend's feet were securely planted deep in the sludge. As Jursic's weight shifted from side to side, Nathan witnessed the man's knee twist and bend unnaturally. Jursic bellowed a sharp, painful cry. Bowing forward to clutch his leg, he lost the fight for balance and fell face first into the muck. Nathan and Mac squirmed trying to turn and offer whatever help they could, but their efforts were too late. Gravity clutched Jursic's large body and propelled him downhill like a gigantic snowball right into Mac. Nathan dropped to his hands and knees doing his best to crawl out of the path of tumbling bodies. In a split second, they were on him. Nathan threw himself forward into the muck hoping the avalanche of men and sludge would roll over the top of him. Instead, he was caught up in the forward momentum and helplessly tumbled head over heels until he hit the bottom of the slope. In the few moments it had taken to cascade all the way down the ridge, the unforgiving clay-like mud had covered their bodies.

Splayed out spread eagle on his back, Nathan's face was also awash with mud that might as well have been glue. He had to open his lips to breathe. Sputtering on the muck, he blew it out of his mouth. Covered head to toe in the gooey concrete-like sludge, he was stuck where he landed. Taking stock of the situation, the first thing he noticed was the muffled sound of Jursic's short raspy gasps for breath. Squirming, he tried to wriggle his way free. Grunting from the effort, he rolled left and then right fighting to free his arms from the jacket that was now another casualty of the wilderness. Sitting with his legs stretched out in front of him, Nathan flapped his hands to remove clumps of mud and wiped his face. Finally, able to see, he readied himself to kick Jursic's ass while struggling to get on his hands and knees. A loud ripping noise stopped him dead in his tracks. The sludge had just claimed its next victim—his pants. Defeat washed over him. He dropped his head and wailed, "What else can possibly go wrong? Give me a fucking break!"

A deep guttural moan stopped his crippling feelings of utter demoralization in their tracks. Jursic was in excruciating pain and needed help. That was the kick in the ass Nathan needed to override the despair of defeat.

Jursic's bright white teeth were bared in a painful grimace. They were the only part of his body that wasn't coated in a thick layer of mud.

Crawling through the muck proved even more difficult than walking. Each movement pulled at Nathan's shredded clothing. His ripped pants were a hindrance, so he fought to escape them. Retrieving his gun and phone which now resembled the mud pies of his youth, he scurried on his hands and knees to Jursic's side.

Wiping the filth from his friend's eyes, he asked, "How bad is it?"

Jursic couldn't talk. He pitched from side to side burying his large body deeper into the quagmire.

Mac sidled up beside them and grabbed one of Jursic's arms to help work him free. Nathan took one look at the rancher, and the ridiculousness of the situation prompted a laugh. The man hadn't fared any better than he had. Mac had lost every stitch of clothing too. There was no sign of his revolver, but he held tight to his now nonfunctional mud-covered long gun.

"Jursic, we've got to move. Come on. Nathan will take one side, and I'll take the other."

Just as they gained their footing a loud noise over the ridge caught their attention. Not having a clue what to expect next, both Mac and Nathan forced Jursic's big body behind them to protect him from this new intrusion and possible threat. With their weapons rendered useless, they had no way to defend themselves. The top of the old cedar whipped in all directions at once. The memory of being trapped inside the line shack as a gruesome creature tried to smoke them out with gusts of wind from its large wings ran through Nathan's mind. *Shit! What now!*

Whomp. Whomp. Whomp. The helicopter breached the ridge and breezed over them, landing on more stable, rockier ground in the distance. Finally, things were starting to go their way. Giddy now, Nathan clutched Jursic's shoulders and shook his friend. "Well, I'll be damned." Nathan glanced at Mac and grinned. "I just figured out who Spirit Talker and her man are. My partner, Jared, is married to Jody, the woman I was telling you about last night. She's a medium. Spirit Keeper must've given her the Spirit Talker moniker." Nathan threw his head back and cackled. "Hot damn! We're safe!"

Getting back to the business at hand, Nathan reached out for his friend. "Come on, Jursic. We've got to get out of this muck. We're going to Flagstaff in style."

By the time the men reached the Bastion Enterprises helicopter, each forced movement trudging through the sludge had tested their endurance to the extreme.

Jared opened the door to their means of escape and all but tumbled out howling with laughter. "When Spirit Keeper said you needed to be rescued, finding you playing in the mud was never on my radar." He bent and slapped his thighs. "At first sight, you all look like an impressive herd of bigfoot."

"Ha, ha. Very fucking funny. Move over and let us in."

Jared blocked the door and crossed his arms. "I've got space blankets. Every one of you is going to have to wipe yourselves down and wrap up before you get into this helicopter."

Fully aware of the dangers surrounding them, Nathan and his mud-buddies wasted no time doing as they were told. Scooping handfuls of mud off of their naked forms only smeared the clay-like substance deeper into their pores. While their bodies were still covered in filth at least they weren't weighted down with heavy clumps. The only way to get clean would be a nice hot shower. Wrapping themselves in the silver blankets that resembled tin foil, Mac and Nathan helped Jursic into the helicopter. Unable to contain the relief at their departure from this miserable land, Nathan threw his head back and roared with laughter. "We look like burritos."

The adrenaline rush of the last several hours was starting to subside. Nervous tension faded to black and left exhaustion in its wake. Pivoting, Nathan shot a fleeting look at the hill they'd just traversed. "Don't get too comfortable. I'll be coming back for you. That's a promise."

Mac leaned toward the pilot and pointed. "On your way in, you flew over a line shack. It's just past that big cedar. Can you hover over it before we leave? Don't go too low. I want to get a look at the roof."

Jared nodded his assent to the pilot, and they were off.

The area surrounding the cabin showed indentations in the mud all the way around the shelter— obvious signs of being trampled. However, it was impossible to determine from the sky if animals or humans caused the destruction. The sheer numbers it would take to wreak that much havoc to the landscape had to be huge. They were disappointed that there was no sign or clue as to what had been on the roof before Spirit Keeper had found them.

From the front seat, Jared twisted around to talk to Nathan. "I don't know what happened to you guys last night but hold your story for now. Spirit Keeper is in a tizzy. He sent word that he's demanding an audience with all of us immediately, and I believe it has to do with whatever you experienced here. The exact words conveyed to me were, '*Go get them and bring them to me. I also want to speak with the witch and Spirit Talker.*' " He chuckled. "You should have seen how Jody beamed when she heard the shaman's name for her."

Nathan opened his mouth to speak, but Mac interrupted. "That's good because I've got a few questions for him myself. Since the man showed up on the rooftop this morning, I'm fairly sure he knows exactly what is going on here and what happened to my men."

Jared's face went blank. "Umm. No. That's impossible. Spirit Keeper is camped up on the peaks just east of Flagstaff because he's coming to the wedding tomorrow. The man doesn't carry a cell phone, so he'd never have been able to make it back in time to send for help."

Nathan adamantly shook his head. "I can't explain it, Jared, but the old man *was* here. He saved us."

Jared's eyebrows rose into his hairline. "Okay." The word sounded more like a question than a statement. "I can't wait to hear *this* story."

Jursic groaned and wiggled, trying to get more comfortable. Jared's attention switched to his new employee. "Jursic, how bad are you hurt?"

"It's nothing."

Nathan rolled his eyes and harrumphed. Removing his hand from the space blanket, he slapped his friend on the arm. "Stop being a damn hero. The injury is bad. I saw his knee bow out when his leg got stuck in the mud. I'm not a doctor, but if I had to guess he probably tore an ACL. He can't put any weight on it."

Disregarding Jursic's reply, Jared continued. "Okay. While Spirit Keeper wanted to meet with all of us, I think it would be prudent to have someone, maybe Amy, take Jursic to the hospital. She's at our house right now cooking for the wedding tomorrow. We'll meet the old man without him. And Jursic?" Jared stared as he waited for the man's reply.

"Yes?"

"I don't know what happened, but everything you've seen and heard is confidential. Do not, I repeat, *do not* share any experiences or feelings with anyone outside of this helicopter. We owe it to our client to get to the bottom of the problem with no publicity. Understood?"

Jursic nodded. "Yes, sir."

Turning to the pilot, Jared concluded, "Land out by the pond on our property. They can wash up in the outdoor shower. Jody will kill me if I let them into the house the way they are."

Chapter Ten

Since Mac didn't have a change of clothing, Jared opened his closet to his guest. On the way back to the outdoor shower, he stopped by the guest cottage and retrieved clothing for Nathan and Jursic from their suitcases.

After the men cleaned up, they helped Jursic to the main house. Amy ran out of the back door and down the steps. "What on earth happened to you, Mr. Jursic?"

His friend, the dolt, shot the woman his million-dollar pretty boy smile. Nathan jabbed him in the side to remind Jursic that this woman was off limits. It had only been two or three months since she and her small child had escaped an abusive husband. "Amy, I've told you a million times none of this mister stuff. Call me Pete or Peter. I'm fine. Really. No need to fuss."

Amy's hands landed soundly on her tiny hips. "Is that so? Then why are you practically being carried by Nathan and..." Only then did she realize that the other man wasn't Jared. Her reaction was typical of an abused woman. She shied away and lowered her eyes. Amy was a strong woman and had come a long way emotionally in the few months she'd been freed from the tragic situation that had been her life. But the effects were still noticeable. Nathan quickly intervened, in an effort to make her feel a little more comfortable. "Amy, meet John MacAllister. Mac, this is Amy. The best damn cook in the state of Arizona."

Amy's shy blush prompted Nathan to grin. He was relieved to see her relax if only a bit. "It's nice to meet you, Mr. MacAllister."

"Pleasure, ma'am."

Jursic shifted his weight and groaned. Amy's full attention was back on the problem at hand. "Is Peter the only one hurt? Or do I need to take a look at all of you?"

Jared barreled out of the house waving a pad of paper and car keys, followed closely by more of the bride's friends and coven mates, Sarah and Camille. "Amy, we have to hurry. Jody is at Spirit Keeper's camp. She just called and he's getting impatient. Would you be able to drive Jursic to the hospital? I'm afraid his injuries are beyond what we can take care of here at the house." Tearing the top sheet from the pad, he handed it off to Amy. "I've called ahead and made arrangements. Just in case there's a problem, give them this note. It covers everything."

"I said I was fine, dammit!" Jursic squawked.

Nathan sucked in a deep breath, and everyone else froze. *That boy is asking for trouble. No one speaks to the boss like that.*

Jared walked to within inches of Jursic and captured him in a steely gaze. "Being new to my organization, I'm going to give you a pass for that little outburst—*this* time. Let me put it this way. You *are* going to the hospital. That is a direct order. Do you understand me?"

Jursic's gaze fell. "Yes, sir. I'm sorry, sir. I just don't like hospitals."

Amy placed Jursic's arm around her slight shoulders and helped stabilize him by wrapping her arm as far around his waist as she could. "If he gives you any guff, Amy, feel free to slap him down. That would be an order if you worked for me. But since you don't, I'm appealing to your maternal instincts."

Beaming, she patted Jursic's back. "Mr. Jursic won't give me any trouble. Because if he does, he won't get any of the chicken fried steak I'd planned on making for dinner. Isn't that right, Peter?"

"Are there going to be mashed potatoes and fried okra too?"

The petite woman beamed up at Jursic. "Yep. But only if you're on your best behavior."

"Lead the way, Amy. I'm your slave. You'll get no trouble from me. I promise."

Nathan took a step forward to intervene, but Jared stopped him. "Let them go. Jursic knows she's fragile. He'll behave himself. She'll be fine."

Sarah rushed forward with a purse the size of a suitcase and threw the bag in the backseat. "Little Marcus is sleeping, so don't worry about him. Me and Camille will keep a close eye on the tot. Take as long as you need."

Nathan continued to watch as she gently tucked Jursic into the car with all the care of a loving mother. Amy embraced Sarah and uttered a swift thank you while jumping into the driver's side.

"She seems perfectly happy. What's wrong with her?" Both Jared and Nathan turned to face the rancher.

Nathan spoke in a low whisper. "She's suffered a serious trauma. Her husband beat her to within an inch of her life. From what we were able to garner, he'd been mistreating her for years.

"Rainy—you'll be meeting her in just a bit—and a few other good-hearted people got her and her son out just in the nick of time."

Nathan couldn't help but notice how Mac's features hardened upon hearing the tragic episode in Amy's life. The car carrying his friend sped down the driveway. The rancher's gaze never left the retreating vehicle until it had sped out of view. "I'd like to get my hands around the throat of a man that hurts a defenseless woman. He deserves…"

Mac trailed off, and Nathan finished the sentence. "Range justice?"

"Yeah. That's how we handle assholes in Montana."

Nathan rubbed his chin to keep the grin hidden. "Someday you're gonna have to clue me in on what range justice is exactly."

Mac offered a sideways smirk but no explanation.

Chapter Eleven

The mood in the car was far too tense. Jared was talking himself blue trying to keep Mac from losing his cool. But Nathan was oddly calm. After Spirit Keeper's appearance last night, he knew the old man would shoot straight and provide answers to their questions. And there were a lot of questions.

Letting his attention wander to Bright Flower, he was certain the woman that plagued his dreams would be at her grandfather's camp. After hearing Mac's story about losing his wife and wasted time, Nathan had come to a decision. Once the business at hand was taken care of, he would discuss the matter of Bright Flower and her choice of groom with her grandfather. He knew it was a long shot, but he had to try.

The twisting dirt road climbed in elevation above the town of Flagstaff. While the snow in town had long since melted, there were still several feet of the white powder covering the mountainside. He'd often in the past visited Snowbowl, one of Arizona's popular ski slopes. But this side of the mountain was more isolated. A man could hike for hours without seeing another soul up here. The scenery was gorgeous, and Nathan vowed to take some time to explore more of the San Francisco Peaks once this mess was concluded.

One last hairpin-turn and the steep terrain morphed

into a large meadow cocooned by snow-covered pines. Tents dotted the landscape. Nathan couldn't believe there were so many people milling about. Children were throwing snowballs, dogs barked in the distance. Women were hovering around large metal pots hanging over several fire pits. It was a small Navajo community that had traveled with their holy man, probably to ensure his safety. The scene playing out in front of Nathan left him breathless and yearning for a simpler lifestyle. *Home*, he thought. *Family. A man's dreams could be fulfilled living a simpler life like this with the right woman.*

Nathan's friends were sitting on blankets around a blazing fire pit smack dab in the middle of the camp. Jody was the first to stir, as she sauntered to Jared's side. The couple shared a kiss. Terry greeted Nathan as his bride-to-be, Rainy, stepped forward and whispered, "I'm glad you're finally here. Spirit Keeper is nervous about something. He's been very mysterious and refused to offer any insight until you arrived. And by the way, Bright Flower is looking as beautiful as ever." Giggling, Rainy kissed his cheek. With one eyebrow cocked, she just had to get in one last dig. "Tick-tock."

Bright Flower stood on the other side of the fire pit brandishing a beautiful smile. She was magnificent. Their last embrace in his dream flashed across Nathan's mind. *Oh, yeah. I'll fight for her.* His field of vision sharpened and zeroed in on her—leaving everyone else forgotten. There was no more disputing the obvious. The striking Indian princess was his. He refused to live with the regrets of what could have been if he didn't make a move.

Stepping closer, reality slapped Nathan in the face

when Spirit Keeper's sharp voice penetrated his hazy mind. "Sit, granddaughter." The old man never moved and continued to gaze into the sparking flames. His flat tone offered no clue as to his intent.

Nathan had to get a hold of himself. There was other business that needed resolving before he could discuss his future with the old man's granddaughter. He glanced away to gain a little perspective when he realized the tribesmen and women who'd moments ago been circulating throughout the camp had disappeared, leaving them to conduct their business in privacy.

Weary and concerned for his men, Mac's agitation was evident in the way he clenched his teeth and fisted his hands. They were all aware Spirit Keeper had the answers, but Nathan didn't want to ruffle the old man's feathers. They may never find out what was going on if they weren't diplomatic. Crouching beside Spirit Keeper as the others took their places around the fire, Nathan greeted the old man. "Sir, it's nice to see you again. Thank you for inviting us to your camp."

Spirit Keeper nodded. Nathan glanced at Bright Flower. "It's nice to see you again. We appreciate your hospitality."

A corner of her mouth rose as she responded, "You and your friends are always welcomed by our fire."

The dreams with Bright Flower had taught Nathan that her people were prideful. He wanted to make every effort to gain the old man's trust. "Sir, I'd like to introduce you to John MacAllister. He owns the land that you visited last night. We all offer thanks for saving our hides." Bright Flowers's posture stiffened, and she jerked her head toward her grandfather, her brow deeply ridged. Taken aback, Nathan realized she must not have known why they were there.

Spirit Keeper glanced up and acknowledged the rancher's presence with a slight tilt of the head. "Sit by my fire. We have much to discuss." Appeased somewhat, Mac nodded curtly and squatted directly across the flames from the medicine man.

Nathan breathed a sigh of relief when the rancher acquiesced without a sign of contention. He could see the anger boiling just below the surface in the man's taut facial features, but he was allowing Nathan to take the lead—at least for now. "Sir, I believe you brought us here to—"

Spirit Keeper's hand flew into the air and curtly cut Nathan off. "There is business we must discuss before we can resolve the problems of last night. I must know. Are you planning on asking for my granddaughter?"

Taken completely off guard, Nathan's eyes widened in surprise. "Well, I—I mean, I wasn't—I thought…"

"Enough." The old man spoke sharply. "For years my granddaughter has spoken about a bilagáana—a white man—that she was destined to be joined with. Given her position with our people, naturally, I dismissed those thoughts as the wild ramblings of a young child. I thought surely with age she'd drop the subject. But over a period of many years, she has continued to profess a budding relationship through dream travel."

Nathan looked at Bright Flower inquisitively. "*Years?* No. I mean, I will admit that after meeting your granddaughter at Jared and Jody's wedding, I haven't been able to stop thinking about her. She's always on my mind, even in sleep. But the dreams started *after*

Jody and Jared's wedding."

Spirit Keeper smirked. "Tell me, Nathan, as a child, the majority of your dreams were never revealed to you, were they?" Slack-jawed Nathan stared at the old man wondering how this conversation had deviated so far off the mark. He wasn't ready to discuss the subject of Bright Flower yet. He certainly didn't want to do it in front of all of these people.

The old man pursed his lips. "Many a morning you awoke having no clue what had transpired in your sleep. True?"

Nathan's mind worked feverishly to keep up. *How in the hell would this old man know that it was a rare occasion for me to remember dreams as a child?* Rubbing his brow, he decided the best course of action would be to get it over with and just answer the question truthfully. "Well, yes, sir, that's correct. I have no memory of most of my childhood dreams."

A disembodied throaty snort beside Nathan startled him. Reaching up to cover his ear, he could've sworn he felt the hot breath of a huge animal bearing down on him. Losing his balance, he fell off of his haunches onto his ass. *What the hell?* Staring at the empty space beside him, he could swear the guttural grunt he'd just heard was that of the buffalo in his dreams.

Spirit Keeper's features softened as a bright, pleasure-filled smile blossomed. "You can hear your spirit animal. That's good to know."

Nathan struggled to keep his features steady. The old man was obviously bats. "Excuse me, sir? I have no idea what you are talking about. I promise to discuss spirit animals and dreams, and whatever else you'd like at length after the problem at hand is—"

Spirit Keeper grunted. "We will discuss it now. According to my granddaughter from the time you were a boy, her soul traveled and joined you in your dreams. You do not remember because you had not journeyed with her. Your soul remained within your body. It is my opinion that the Creator did not believe that you were ready to glimpse your future. Or perhaps, the Holy One was waiting to see if you would grow into a man *worthy* of your future. When your soul and that of my Bright Flower made the journey together, you were dream questing collectively. Only then were you granted recall. She has told me that she is teaching you our ways."

"I…well…yes. She is a wonderful teacher." Nathan ran his fingers through his hair. He was becoming more confused by the minute. "But, sir, I don't understand the term *dream questing*. What does that mean?"

Rainy, being the High Priestess of the local Wiccan coven, seemed to grasp what the old man was saying and excitedly joined the conversation. "Are you saying that Bright Flower astral projected into Nathan's dreams as a child? And once they met in person, they both traveled through time and space together as they slept?"

Spirit Keeper's head bobbed.

Nathan couldn't hide his confusion. "Dream quest? Astral projection? Travel through time and space?" *What is this nonsense?*

Rainy reached out and grasped Nathan's hand. Their fingers tangled. "It means, my dear friend, that each night your soul leaves your body and joins with Bright Flower's."

Nathan's eyes grew bigger as he stared at Rainy. His heart started to pound. "The dreams are real?"

"Yes. Your soul is tethered to your physical body by a spiritual umbilical cord, but your essence *does* leave and commingles with Bright Flower's. You *weren't* dreaming. You and Bright Flower spent hours upon hours together traveling and learning about each other. The time you were together in your dream quests was as real as if the two of you were in your physical forms in the same room."

Awed, Rainy faced Spirit Keeper. "I knew their bond was a strong one, but I had no clue their joined abilities had progressed to this stage."

The old man folded his arms across his chest. If Nathan were a betting man, he'd say the Indian was impressed.

"It *is* a good match." Bright Flower's grandfather offered a quick head bob and wink to confirm his feelings. "If Nathan were Navajo, he'd be a Singer *and* a witch, just as my granddaughter is. He also has the makings of a strong warrior. They will produce powerful children together." Pleased with his findings, the old man looked first to his granddaughter and then to Nathan.

The praise left Nathan stunned. Thank God Rainy continued to speak on his behalf because he was a complete wreck. He had no clue about any of this. "The Navajo Way of things is different from the European way, Spirit Keeper. As you are well aware, we no longer share in the belief of arranged marriages. It takes time for a couple to develop the type of love needed to result in a happy life-long marriage. Certainly, you cannot expect Nathan to follow Navajo traditions. I agree with you. This match *is* a good one—a strong one and if allowed time, I'm sure it would flourish. But these are not decisions that should be made lightly. From the moment I met Nathan, I knew he was a man of honor and loyalty. I also knew he was the perfect love match for Bright Flower. But the decision is his, and he must have time to make the right one. These things cannot be rushed. It's simply not *our* way."

Annoyed with the dialog, he raised a finger and sliced it through the air to cut her off. The old man turned and scrutinized Nathan. "I've had my doubts, but there are strange and evil doings in the mix. You shared a dream quest last night with my granddaughter that put her life in peril. You have forced my hand. It is time that I step in and make things right. There are secrets— terrible secrets—that I have not shared with another soul. Before these heinous crimes against nature are divulged, Bright Flower needs a man that will protect her with his life if necessary. After last night, I believe *you* are that man, Nathan. Your courage is strong." Spirit Keeper grunted and hit his chest with a closed fist. "We cannot discuss any of the evildoings until my granddaughter has married. Will you be that man? Or shall I call upon another?"

Nathan thought back to the regrets he'd had the previous evening when he was certain death was inevitable. He opened his mouth to speak, but Mac interrupted. "This is crazy! Have you lost your mind, old man? I know you have the answers to what is happening on my land. Are you seriously expecting this man to marry a woman he doesn't know just so you will give us the answers I'm demanding? Answers that I deserve. Again, you're out of your—"

"Enough! Time is short. I must stop hiding and reverse the damage done so many years ago. If Nathan does not accept my granddaughter as his wife, then she will marry another today."

Bright Flower's shocked gasp was ignored by Spirit Keeper. "Either way, we will stop the evil on your land once and for all or die trying. I insist that my granddaughter have the protection of a mate before we continue. The man she takes as a husband must have a warrior spirit. I will not reveal the source of evil until I feel confident that you are all here without judgment. My granddaughter is unaware of the darkness we are facing. There are secrets that must come into the light—secrets that will be painful for my beloved granddaughter."

Spirit Keeper glared at Nathan and all but snarled, "Will you take Bright Flower as a wife right now—or will she marry another?"

Rainy stood and started to object, but Nathan stopped her. He turned and faced the old man. "May I have a few private moments with Bright Flower, sir?"

Spirit Keeper's eyes narrowed as if looking for some sort of trickery. "For what purpose?"

Nathan tried to contain his surprise at the venomous punch behind the question. "With all due respect, sir, the conversation I want to have with your granddaughter is private."

Spirit Keeper tapped Bright Flower's knee and spoke in Navajo. She responded with a curt bob of the head and stood. His beautiful Indian princess walked proudly to Nathan's side.

Guiding her just out of hearing range, Nathan stood in front of her. "Look at me."

Without hesitation, Bright Flower peered up into his eyes. Nathan wanted so badly to wrap her in an embrace but remained still. Fearful of her response, he needed to make sure this marriage was what she wanted because he wouldn't be able to let her go once they'd wed. "Do you agree to this marriage?"

"I do."

"But you are being pressured into this."

She giggled, and a bit of the weight of the moment subsided. Nathan remembered their last kiss in his dream and had to restrain from reaching out to Bright Flower.

"Nathan, I asked you last night in our dream quest if you were planning on ending the torture any time soon. Don't you remember? I've waited a lifetime for you to find me."

A flash of pain flitted in her eyes. Unable to hold his stare, she lowered her gaze. Bright Flower queried barely above a whisper, "Is this what you want, Nathan? Are *you* being pressured? Do you want to marry me?"

He held his hand out, and she latched onto his palm. "I want this more than you can imagine. Let's go tell your grandfather before he brings another man into the mix."

Returning to the campsite, Nathan became aware of his friends' concerned glances. He smiled to ease the tension.

"Spirit Keeper, I will be honest with you. Something happened to me when I met Bright Flower." He rubbed the space over his heart and thumped his chest with his fist. "In here.

"I have not come to you sooner because I did not

feel worthy. But if Bright Flower will have me as a husband, I will protect her with my life. I will love her for eternity."

Spirit Keeper stood and offered his hand to Bright Flower. A stream of tears rolled down the curve of her cheeks. She peered into Nathan's eyes, professing her love for all to see. His dreams were coming true.

"Bright Flower, will you accept this man as your husband?"

"Yes, grandfather."

"Please, everyone stand. Our time is short. Bright Flower, take your place next to your man."

Spirit Keeper took a moment to glance at all of the witnesses. "Given the gravity of the situation, this will not be a traditional ceremony. I will call upon the Creator to bless and join this couple, and then we must move on to more difficult topics."

Unable to believe the turn of events, Nathan gazed into Bright Flower's eyes. His thumb grazed her rounded cheek to wipe her joyful tears. At that moment, he knew he'd do anything in his power to make her happy.

Nathan pivoted to face Spirit Keeper. Unsure of protocol and the consequences of interrupting, he decided to risk those penalties and more for his bride. "Excuse me, sir. Will it be possible to have a traditional service after our business has concluded? I want Bright Flower to have whatever her heart desires, and I believe she would like a proper, traditional Navajo wedding."

Spirit Keeper's hardened features softened. "This *is* a good match." Beaming at Nathan the old man nodded.

"All right, then." Glancing back at the woman who'd claimed his heart, Nathan smiled. "Let's do this."

Bright Flower's grandfather stood proud and tall facing the couple while beating an ancient looking handmade drum. Before long, he started to sing in his native language. The song was hauntingly beautiful. Not having a clue as to what he was chanting, Nathan closed his eyes and lost himself in the resonance. He pictured the old man's words floating on a breeze to the heavens. To the Creator. Power pulsed through every fiber of his being. He didn't know what produced that electric surge of pure energy—if it was Spirit Keeper's song or the woman he stood next to—but marrying Bright Flower was the right thing to do. He'd stand by this woman's side for eternity proving his love and devotion to her.

This ceremony may not be the wedding he thought he'd have, but every melodic note sealed his soul to this woman.

Before long, Bright Flower's fingers curled into his. Nathan looked down into her smiling eyes as the woman he loved spoke to him for the first time as his wife. "You are my husband now. Will you kiss me in front of all of these people?" She stood on tiptoe and puckered up. He bent to take her mouth. This was their first kiss beyond the dream realm. It was familiar. It was right. It was home.

Chapter Twelve

Spirit Keeper's hand disappeared into a pouch. When he drew it out, he tossed a handful of something that appeared to be dried herbs into the fire—provoking a burst of flame and sparks. "We are up against potent dark forces. To succeed I will need the cooperation of the witch and Spirit Talker. We will fail without them."

Locking eyes with Rainy, the old man's stony features never wavered. "You will be married tomorrow, Sunday. It is in our best interest to move quickly. Through vision quest, the Creator has spoken to me. Mid-day on the following day, the sun will die and be reborn. It will be neither day nor night. The solar eclipse is an offering from the Underworld to rid blackness from the earth and restore peace to the land and our Navajo people. I have been granted a revelation and believe that Monday is the day we *must* move forward. What I will be asking of you is extremely dangerous. Can I count on your support and that of your man?"

Holding Terry's hand, Rainy looked to him for consent. He nodded solemnly. She offered her husband-to-be a beautiful smile and caressed his cheek. Turning back to Spirit Keeper her head dipped in approval. "It would be a privilege to help you. We're in."

Spirit Keeper's attention shifted to Jody. "Spirit

Talker, we will not succeed without your gifts. I will not lie. The bond between you and your man is strong. In all of my years, I've never seen the likes of it before. The magic the two of you offer is powerful. I believe that is why the Creator put you in our path. If you consent, your lives *will* be in jeopardy from a magic darker than you could imagine. Will you and your man join your friends and support this cause to help us cleanse evil from this place?"

Jody peered deeply into Jared's eyes looking for any sign of disapproval. When he offered a tense smile, she leaned in and kissed him. "My husband and I will be proud to help in any way we can."

"John MacAllister, you are the owner of the cursed land. There is much at stake for you and your legacy. You sit here at my fire respectfully as we discuss taboos foreign to you. As of yet, you have not passed judgment. I believe you to be a man of principles and a good warrior. I would be honored if you joined us in this battle."

Mac tilted his head. "I will do everything in my power to help clear the land of this malignancy. Whatever it may be."

"Then let us proceed with the details." Spirit Keeper reached out for Bright Flower's hand—one last reassurance before he continued with his story. For the first time since arriving, Nathan glimpsed frailty within the man.

"My sweet child, we are dealing with two separate problems. One you are aware of, the other you are not. I had hoped that you would never learn of the events I am about to tell you." Spirit Keeper cleared his throat and hesitated. "Bright Flower, unpleasant events mar our past and bring shame to our family. Only the elders in our community know of what I'm about to speak. The time has come for me to right a wrong that occurred many years before your birth.

"Before I start, though, I must explain a few things to your husband and the rancher. They are not familiar with our ways and traditions, so I must speak the uncomfortable truth about the cursed land."

Bright Flower nodded her approval.

Looking to Nathan, Spirit Keeper continued, "There are tightly held secrets that are familiar to only Native American tribes. The curse with which I am about to speak of was brought about by all tribes across the country several hundred years ago. Today, the terms of the curse may seem harsh, but it was the way of things back then to protect our people.

"In the many years before my birth, there were locations scattered across the country that housed the unwanted. The land you were on last night is one of those areas. It is why the territory has never been profitable or inhabitable.

"For as long as my people have traveled this earth, the land you occupy has been a prison for those touched in the head and heart. They were shunned and sent to that place to live out the rest of their lives and to die a solitary death. No one grieved their loss. No one shared in their misery. They simply stopped existing the moment they were cast out. Once driven onto that property, there was no means of escape. Powerful wards were placed to hold the living and dead within the boundaries. Besides those touched in the head and body, dangerous men and woman who refused to follow our ways were sent there to be forever locked away from the tribe's population. Once dead, their spirits cannot escape. They walk the ground within the boundaries of the wards forever, never to be granted access to the Underworld.

"This is a taboo subject that is known by all but never discussed out loud. The fact that I am telling you about this shows you that I am willing to do what I can to reverse the curse and release the spirits to the Underworld.

"As you can imagine, this will be a difficult task." Spirit Keeper looked directly at Mac. "After the curse is lifted, there will be offerings you must make every full moon. My granddaughter will advise you on such matters when the time comes."

The old man gazed into the fire, seemingly hesitant to continue. Rocking back and forth, the holy man shivered. "There is something far more dangerous than the curse that thrives on that land which must be dealt with before there can be peace. The barriers are weakening and not strong enough to cage its power much longer.

"Over the years, I have taken it upon myself to fight this evil. Through dream quest, I have secretly traveled to the cursed land many times with my spirit animal. That is how I came upon you, Nathan, where you were under siege in that small cabin. Spirit Keeper paused while he swayed back and forth—his gaze catching others besides Nathan's. "I've had no success in culling the danger. Even with the Creator's help, I am not strong enough to dispatch the evil alone.

"The Creator has offered us the blessing of three minutes—the moment of the sun's rebirth—to dispatch the evil. My people have long since been fearful of the eclipse and marked its time with seclusion within their homes. It is my belief that the roaming spirits of the dead will be left powerless at this time."

Distressed by his discomfort, Bright Flower laid her hand on Spirit Keeper's arm. "I don't understand, Grandfather. What could be more dangerous than imprisoned spirits?"

The old man's face slackened. He seemed miles away. The fire popped and brought him back into focus. He lifted his eyes and intentionally met everyone's stare once again. "I am a Navajo singer—a holy man. I am also a witch. Navajo magic is not the same as European magic. There are four types of Navajo witchcraft used in our religion, only one of which my granddaughter and I practice—the Frenzy Way. We use charms and chants with this type of magic to help heal the hearts, minds, and bodies of our tribesmen.

"There are practitioners with dark hearts that use the other three Ways—those that carry greed and malevolence within their souls. I will not bore you with the details behind the magical ways of my people at this time, except I must discuss the Witchery Way." Bright Flower gasped and her hands flew to her mouth. Nathan felt her shiver and pulled her close.

"When I was a boy, someone extremely powerful used this form of dangerous magic to hex your property—the land of the shunned spirits."

Moved by his granddaughter's reaction, Spirit Keeper captured and held her in his gaze. "Please forgive me, my child, for I have not been honest with you. I had a brother. A twin."

Rainy jerked in surprise and struggled to catch her breath. Her raspy gasp drew everyone's attention.

Jumping to her feet, she crossed the distance to the old man. She clearly had some understanding of the situation that baffled the rest of the people in attendance. Embracing the holy man, she reached out and touched Bright Flower's arm offering comfort. "Spirit Keeper, is your brother still alive?"

A frown creased his face. "Yes."

Bright Flower covered her ears. "No!" Her head jerked back as if she'd been struck. Her eyes practically bulged from their sockets as her breathing became labored. The silence around the fire was deafening. Wanting to comfort his new wife but not having a clue as to why this was unwelcome news, Nathan snapped, "Why does hearing this disturb Bright Flower? I would think it's a good thing to find out you have more family. *What* is the problem?"

The old man was rendered speechless. Bright Flower pressed into Nathan's side and answered his question through sobs. "Grandfather and I come from a long line of powerful singers. There is only one reason this man lives, and I was not aware of his existence. His heart is black, and he uses his power for himself instead of others. He walks the wrong path." Her final words were barely audible.

"Oh my God." Rainy reached for the pentacle encircling her neck and closed her eyes while reciting some sort of protection chant. Seemingly gathering strength from the action, she spoke in a loud, clear tone. "This is not your fault, Spirit Keeper. We are here to help right this terrible wrong. Tell us everything so that we may fight and win this battle."

The holy man's spine stiffened as he gathered himself. "I will not state his name. Doing so may benefit him.

"We were sixteen when I first noticed the blackness of his heart. He'd harmed a young girl and claimed it was his right. Even at such a young age, he felt—no—he believed that all women should kneel to him and praise him for his power. My *brother*," the word dripped in venom, "demanded payment over and above what was right for performing healing rituals. If the tribesmen refused, he'd curse them and send them to a painful death.

"When our father heard of this betrayal, he beat him to within an inch of his life. He told my brother that if he continued to turn toward evil, he would banish him and send him to the cursed land to die.

"That night when all in the house were asleep, my brother killed my mother and father. I was out with friends that evening, or he would have slaughtered me as well. He waited in the shadows for me to return. He jumped me as I approached the house and would have killed me, but I got a lucky punch in and knocked him out.

"I didn't know what to do. I was crazy with fear. Finally, I ran to the elders and told them what had happened. My brother was gone by the time we returned.

"He feeds off of fear. I've heard stories of visitations from a man that travels in and out of the cursed land wearing the skin of a coyote and a headdress made from owl feathers."

Bright Flower shrieked and jumped to her feet. She ran for the edge of the woods and threw herself to the ground. Her body violently spasmed as she heaved the contents of her stomach. Nathan was by her side in an instant. He wiped her face and pulled her onto his lap. She cowered in his embrace and wailed, "I'm so sorry, Nathan. I'm so sorry. My family has brought great shame to you and yours. I will understand if you no longer wish to be married to me. It was wrong of Grandfather not to disclose this terrible secret before we joined in marriage."

Cupping her face, he touched his nose to hers. "I have no idea what has you so upset, but you are my wife, and I will not allow you to say such things. What could you possibly be sorry for, baby? You've done nothing wrong," he cooed.

Rainy and Jody knelt beside them. Frustrated with the lack of answers, Nathan queried, "Rainy, you seem to have an understanding of what Spirit Keeper is saying. Would you please explain it to me because I'm clueless?"

There was no way to read Rainy's stone-faced expression. "It's not mine to tell. We must go back to the fire and hear the rest."

Brushing loose hair away from Bright Flower's face, Rainy spoke in a calming but demanding tone, "Bright Flower, I know this is a lot to take in, but the only way we're going to defeat this is to know everything. None of this is your fault. None of this is your grandfather's fault. We are dealing with a demented soul that has the power to ruin your people and mine alike. We must defeat him. Now, get yourself together and let's go finish this."

Nathan grabbed Rainy's arm and swung her around. "I don't understand. *What* is happening?"

Dark shadows in Rainy's eyes showed just how desperate the situation was. "I'm not going to lie,

Nathan. This is bad. It's the worst-case scenario. There are some things in the Navajo culture that are truly terrifying. We are about to confront the worst of the worst. Now, come on. Let's get back to the fire." She folded her arms around herself and shivered. "Spirit Keeper will inform you of what we are facing."

Once everyone had rejoined the circle, all eyes were trained on Spirit Keeper. The fire flared and popped as if it were directly affected by the nervous tension surrounding the group.

"It is said in the Navajo culture that for one to achieve ultimate evil, a person must destroy their humanity. There are several ways for one so inclined to do this. The wicked act of..." Spirit Keeper pursed his lips and glanced at his granddaughter. He spoke in rapid Navajo. Bright Flower appeared to be in deep thought when she looked to Nathan. "What is the English word for killing your parents?"

His heart was breaking for her. "Parricide."

Spirit Keeper continued. "Yes. Parricide is the ultimate way to destroy a Navajo's humanity. To inaugurate yourself into the Navajo magic of Witchery Way you must have a malignant heart."

The old man was speaking in riddles and starting to annoy Nathan. Still not grasping the full scope of the situation, he inquired, "Sir, I'm sorry, but I'm having a tough time understanding what this has to do with the MacAllister land."

"Through the magic of Witchery Way, my brother wears the pelt of a coyote and the feathers of an owl. He lives and breathes but is no longer human. He is a powerful skinwalker."

It was Mac's turn to interrupt. "Skinwalker? I've

never heard of that term. What does it mean?"

"Through the Witchery Way magic, my brother draws on the power of the coyote and the owl to shift into an abomination—a cross between the two. When you and the other men were attacked at the cabin, my brother was on the roof."

Nathan shivered when he thought back to the eerie sounds the animal made that night—a cross between a dog and a raptor.

Mac leaned forward and spoke directly to Nathan. "Is he talking about shapeshifters? Do you believe this?"

An internal battle was settling squarely in Nathan's brain. Did he believe in shapeshifters? Before last night the answer would have been an unequivocal no. But now? After everything he went through yesterday, his mind was coming around to a more open way of looking at the situation.

"Take into consideration our experiences while we were on your land—feeling watched, no wildlife to speak of, all of the artifacts we came across, the compass. The curse with cast out spirits makes a lot of sense to me. Over my lifetime, I've found that you don't have to believe in things for them to be real." Nathan's attention turned to Spirit Keeper. "I'm still confused as to what role your brother plays in all of this?"

Rainy spoke up. "It's the cast out spirits. He wants their souls. They are his army."

Nathan whipped his gaze back to Spirit Keeper. The old man nodded and said, "Yes. You are correct. Through the Witchery Way, he's raised the dead, and they are now his puppets. The cast out spirits were angry, and he's used that to turn them into his slaves. They want revenge. My brother has been trying for years to break the barriers of the cursed land. He wants to free his warriors on society. I fear that he is getting close. If he cannot be stopped, it will not be long before the abominations he's created—half human, half monster—are unleashed on my people."

Nathan pondered this for a moment and then asked, "What exactly does a shapeshifter do? What harm does it cause? What are the dangers?"

"You must never show fear when near a skinwalker. The dead feed on the negative emotion. They will take all of your energy and leave only a shell behind. Ultimately you will die a hideous death.

"You must never hold the gaze of a skinwalker. They will invade your body and use it at will. They will be happy with nothing less than full possession. These creatures cannot live among humans without being detected. Their best bet for living in society would be to take a host body. If these monsters cannot be stopped, this will most likely be the outcome of the spirit skinwalkers we will be facing. They want to walk with the living again. In doing so, they can cause complete devastation."

"Not only is my brother a powerful shapeshifter, but he has also raised the dead and bargained with the spirits offering freedom from eternal confinement. I'm afraid there are many spirits on the cursed land that no longer have any human thoughts or cares. In your culture, they would be called demons.

"I am ashamed. For years, I have been prideful and thought I could contain my brother and his evildoings. But repeatedly I have failed. I see now that the only way to remove the danger is with the help of the people sitting around this fire. If we continue with our plan to attack, many steps must be taken before Monday."

Spirit Keeper's gaze settled on each guest around his fire before speaking again. "After hearing the threat, are you all still prepared to join forces to destroy the enemy?"

Each person solemnly nodded.

"Good." The old man looked at Rainy and Terry. "You two will marry tomorrow. Fill your hearts with laughter. Enjoy your guests and celebration for it is full hearts with love and laughter and joy that will help crush the enemy.

"After the festivities, Nathan and Bright Flower will meet me here at my camp." Spirit Keeper held his arms out and stated, "This mountain is sacred to my people. This is a good place for learning our ways. There is much I must teach my grandson before we go into battle.

"At dawn on Monday, I will meet each of you at the place the witch and her man join to discuss each person's role in the battle. The wedding circle holds joyful vibrations. That land and all of its memories of sacred bonds will give us the courage and power to defeat our enemy. Bring all of your weapons and ammunition to that place. To be effective against our spirit enemies, our tools of war must be anointed. I will perform a spiritual cleansing and protection ceremony.

"Time grows short. I must consult with the Creator. But before I do, I would request a private word with Mr. MacAllister and my grandson."

Stunned by the revelations, everyone stood. Bright Flower helped her grandfather up, and Spirit Keeper declared, "Granddaughter, see to the comfort of our guests until we return. Gentlemen, if you will follow me, please."

****

An hour passed before the men rejoined the circle around the campfire. The camp had come alive again. Children chased dogs. Women bent over their cooking pots. The communal festivities continued as if evil had no hold on the future of those gathered together.

On the inside, Nathan's emotions were raging and tore at him with doubts, feelings of betrayal, and fear. Unable to share Spirit Keeper's secrets with the others, Nathan did his best to remain stoic. Glancing at Bright Flower—the woman of his dreams—he prayed that her grandfather's wishes wouldn't destroy his marriage before it even began.

Chapter Thirteen

An uncomfortable silence plagued the car's occupants since they'd left Spirit Keeper's camp. Nathan's emotions were all over the place. He'd suffered through the highest of highs and the lowest of lows today, and those frenetic emotions had left him feeling numb.

Peering into the rearview mirror, he found Mac lost in thought and gazing out the side window. *I can't imagine what the man is feeling or thinking right now.* He flicked the blinker on and reached for Bright Flower's hand. Giving it a little squeeze for reassurance, he said, "This has been a rollercoaster day. The time has come to relax and enjoy the company of good people. Amy has prepared a feast as a wedding present for Rainy and Terry. I've been looking forward to this meal all week."

Glancing back into the mirror, Nathan winced at the scowl on Mac's face. "I know that you're under a lot of pressure—and probably not feeling very sociable—but this is an opportunity to get to know the people who are going to help with your problem. At least stay downstairs for supper. I promise you, if nothing else, Amy's cooking will go a long way to putting you in a better frame of mind."

Jody and Jared's cabin lights flashed in the

distance through the tall trees. One last turn and the Ponderosa Pine opened up to the meadow used for parking. Jursic had perched himself on the front porch. Nathan parked the vehicle and turned the ignition off. Once he, his new bride, and Mac exited the car, he offered a two-finger salute to his friend when the man stood, with the aid of crutches to greet them.

"It looks like the pre-wedding dinner party is in full swing," Nathan said, relieved that he wouldn't be the only person trying to spark up a conversation with Mac. If all else failed, he'd be willing to bet Jursic could loosen the rancher up with a little twisted humor and a beer or two.

Soft music played in the background and laughter resonated from inside the home. Brandishing a huge smile, his friend and co-worker hobbled toward the car. Nathan queried, "So what's the verdict on your knee?"

He lifted his shoulders as if to soften the news. "You were right. It's a torn ACL. I've got to have surgery next week."

Before Nathan could respond, Mac stepped forward and held his hand out. "I'm sorry you were injured on my property. I feel responsible. I appreciate everything you've tried to do for me. I'd be obliged if you'd allow me to pay your hospital bill."

Jursic accepted Mac's hand and shook it soundly. "No need, sir. Bastion Enterprises is covering everything. Please, come and join the group inside. You look like you could use a beer."

"You have no idea."

Mac headed for the front porch as Jursic's attention turned back to Nathan and the woman at his side. The moment he recognized Bright Flower his face lit with a devilish grin. "Well, well, well. I've only seen a drawing of you, but I'd know that beautiful face anywhere. *You* must be Bright Flower. The others said you'd be joining us tonight. Since our mutual friend, here, hasn't introduced us yet, let me do the honors. I'm Pete Jursic. It's a pleasure to finally meet you." His thumb jerked in Nathan's direction. "If it were up to this guy, I think he'd probably keep you all to himself."

Bright Flower beamed. "I'm happy to meet any friend of Nathan's. I'm sure we'll be seeing a lot more of each other."

Let the introductions begin. Nathan cleared his throat knowing full well he'd stomp anyone that put a damper on his wedding night. Securely tucking her into his side, he allowed his delight to shine through his voice. "I'm sorry, sweetheart, let me do this right. Jursic, I'd like you to meet my wife, Bright Flower. Bright Flower, this is Peter Jursic, my friend and partner in crime at work."

Jursic's eyes grew to the size of saucers. Clearly at a loss for words, his mouth gaped open. After a couple of moments of uncomfortable silence, the man seemed to finally focus on Nathan as he offered a genuine smile full of warmth and happiness. "Well, I'll be damned. Congratulations, man!" He reached for Bright Flower's hand. "Normally, the fact that this marriage happened so fast would concern me, but I know how strong Nathan's feelings are for you. I've experienced the brunt of them firsthand. From my heart to yours, thank you. I can guarantee that you've made this guy the happiest man on earth. Now maybe he won't be so distracted or bad-tempered."

He carefully pivoted and started for the cabin.

Glancing over his shoulder, he stated, "By the way, Nathan, your mom is inside. Since Rainy and Terry weren't here, she's been fussing over every wedding detail. Funny thing, I've been with her all afternoon, and she hasn't mentioned a thing about *you* getting married."

Nathan's breath caught in his throat.

Jursic stalled his forward momentum and cackled. "Don't tell me that you got hitched and didn't tell your mom? H-m-m." His friend scratched his chin and continued to goad Nathan. "Well, the good news is that your sisters were a little under the weather, so they decided to stay back at the hotel tonight to avoid getting anyone else sick. At least you won't have to deal with them too." He started to hobble away before calling out, "Let me know if you need me to run interference. Your mom likes me. She's putty in my hands."

Bright Flower appraised her husband's expression as the hold on her hand tightened. His teeth nipped and chewed on his bottom lip. "Nathan, what concerns you? Do you think your mother will object to our marriage?"

He glanced down at her as if he'd momentarily forgotten she was there. Nathan's expression softened as he cupped her face between his two large hands. "No, sweetheart. My mother will love you. I'm a little concerned, because, like you and your grandfather, my family members are close. We share everything. I'm afraid she's going to be hurt that we got married without her being there." Nathan pulled Bright Flower into an embrace. "I feel a little guilty that my family never crossed my mind today. Since we can't tell my mom why the marriage was rushed—at least not yet—I have no idea how I'm going to explain all of this to her."

"Grandfather and I have put you in a terrible position. I don't want to hurt anyone that you love."

Nuzzling the crown of her head, he whispered, "Everything will be okay." But she could tell by his voice that wasn't exactly the truth of the matter.

"You're a good man. I promise to do my best to win her over."

Nathan ran his hands down Bright Flower's back and took a deep breath. "My mom can be a bit of a handful at times. She likes to think she's in charge. I've been single my whole life, so that was never a problem before. I'd just let her have her way because it was easier." Nathan's face contorted with what Bright Flower perceived as full-blown worry. He blew a deep breath out before he continued. "Come on. There's no better time than the present. Let's get this over with."

Each step closer to the cabin became harder. Nathan's anxiety seemed to be catching fire. Upon reaching the front door, Bright Flower jerked his hand from the doorknob. "Wait!" All of a sudden, her stomach twisted in knots. She looked down at her old jeans and scuffed hikers and cringed. "Maybe I should get something more appropriate out of my suitcase and change before I meet your mom? Look at me. I'm a mess."

Nathan bent and kissed her forehead. "Don't be silly. You look beautiful. I didn't mean to scare you. I'm keeping my fingers crossed the famed mother's guilt train doesn't leave the station. If my mom can keep her cool, she'll play nice. If not, she'll just have to come to terms with our marriage on her own. I promise you that I will *not* tolerate one harsh word about you or us."

"I want to make a good impression, Nathan. She's going to think I'm destitute. I don't want to shame you."

He grabbed her shoulders and gently shook her. "Stop that. You are more important to me than anyone on this earth. Hold your head up high and know that you're my woman by choice. You're *my* Native American princess, and I couldn't be prouder of you."

Doing her best to quell her fears, Bright Flower stiffened her spine, threw her shoulders back, and stated with resolve, "All right then. Let's do this."

****

As Bright Flower and Nathan entered the cabin, a tall, plump woman rushed across the room to greet them. She wore a gorgeous teal pantsuit, low heels, and her hair was styled in a chic chignon. *Crap.* Bright Flower's heart sank. Brushing her jean-clad thighs to rid her palms of sweat, she glanced around the spacious area as all conversation came to a halt. Her gaze landed on Jody as the woman offered a wink and a nod of support. Terry stood beside Jody and held his thumb in the air while grinning. He mouthed, *"Everything is going to be okay."*

The weight of the world felt as though it had just landed in the pit of her mid-section. Bright Flower patted her belly to soothe the sensation. All she wanted to do was run and hide.

Bright Flower stood silently by as Nathan's mom reached out and patted his cheek. Her mood appeared jovial. "And just where have you been young man? I haven't heard a word from you in the last three days. I find it ironic that I have to travel one hundred and fifty miles to Flagstaff to see my boy when we both live in the same city."

"Mom," The love and concern in Nathan's voice was evident. "Cut that out. We speak at least twice a week. Why don't we go out back? There's something I'd like to talk to you about."

"Of course, dear." The woman, still apparently unaware of Bright Flower's presence, draped her arm within Nathan's and started for the back door. He reached back and grabbed Bright Flower's hand—towing her along behind them.

Only after the back door shut, was Nathan's mother aware that another person had joined them. Bright Flower stood stock still as the woman appraised her. Offering a slight smile, she said, "Well, hello, darling. You're lovely. Who might you be?"

Bright Flower tried her best to put on a brave front. She only hoped her lips weren't quivering. "Thank you, ma'am. I'm—"

"Oh, please, call me Doris. Are you a friend of my son's?"

"Well—" Bright Flower stuttered.

Nathan, thankfully, picked up the reins and stated, "Mom, I'd like you to meet Bright Flower. We're—"

Doris' excitement spilled out as she clapped her hands and exclaimed, "Don't tell me! You're finally introducing me to one of your girlfriends?" She slapped her son's stomach and Bright Flower flinched. "It's about time!"

Pride gleamed in her eyes as she beamed at Bright Flower. "You have an exotic name, Bright Flower. My boy, here, is quite a catch, young lady. You've certainly got superior taste when it comes to men."

"Mom! Please." He guided her to a bench overlooking the wedding tents. "I don't know how to tell you this, so I'm just going to spit it out. Mom, I married Bright Flower today."

All of the color drained from Doris' face. The smile was still plastered on her lips, but it now appeared forced as if frozen in place. After a few moments, worry lines etched deep into the woman's brow as she stood and wrapped an arm around Bright Flower's shoulders. Tugging to draw her closer, Doris glared directly into her eyes and spat out, "Oh my poor dear. Did this boy of mine get you pregnant?"

Bright Flower gasped, and Nathan yelled, "Mother, stop that right this minute. I will not—"

Bright Flower took the initiative and interrupted Nathan before he said something he'd regret. "Ma'am, I've never been with a man like that. Please don't think badly of your son. He's a man with integrity and would never do such a thing."

Doris' stare was fierce. His mother took a shaky step away. Bright Flower cringed when she realized she'd said something wrong—but for the life of her, she had no idea what that might have been. The woman looked as if she'd blow and turned to vent at Nathan. "I've known you your entire life, young man. I'm your mother for God's sake. What makes this woman think she needs to explain *you* to *me*? Nathan, you need to enlighten me. Are you seriously telling me you married this girl?" The woman's hurt feelings continued to boil over as she let loose the rage and hurt she had to be feeling. Her voice grew louder with each word. "If you didn't marry her out of necessity, why would you do such a thing without telling me? *You're my son.* How on earth could you do this to your sisters and me? Do we mean so little to you?"

Bright Flower didn't know what to feel. Guilt? Anger? Sorrow? She'd never in her life been talked to or about in this manner.

The back doors swung open with a whoosh as Jody and Terry came to the rescue. Jody handed Doris a glass of champagne and smiled sweetly. "Isn't this wonderful news, Doris? Did Bright Flower let you in on the details? I know it must be hard to understand, but the Navajo culture is so much different than ours. Bright Flower wants to have a formal wedding right here where the rest of us have married." Jody glanced apologetically at Bright Flower for her assumptions and winked to help ease the tension. The woman was obviously doing everything in her power to turn this nasty situation around. *Bless her.* As Jody continued to cheerfully chatter at Nathan's mom, Terry guided a stunned and now silent Doris into the house. "You're going to have to put your wedding planner hat on because Bright Flower is going to need your help planning the big event." The door shut soundly behind them.

Nathan pulled her into his arms. They swayed, each allowing the other's embrace to soothe. "I'm sorry my mother said those things to you. She's hurt and lashed out without thinking. She's not angry with you. She's mad at me. We'll give her a little time to adjust to the news. She'll come around. I promise."

Shell shocked, Bright Flower decided a private conversation between her and Doris was necessary—the sooner, the better. She'd wait until after supper and then pull Doris aside and try to ease her concerns.

****

Bright Flower couldn't believe the feast in front of them. Everyone—with the exception of Doris—seemed to talk at the same time, sharing childhood stories and funny tales. Raucous laughter and the joy of being with friends had eased Bright Flower's concerns, for the moment at least. As the evening progressed, and the sting of hurt feelings lapsed, both she and Nathan started to enjoy the pleasure of their first meal as a married couple. They'd shared sideways glances and smiles. She looked at him now and thought her heart might burst with love.

Nathan had offered a bite of his pie, and Bright Flower kindly accepted. Doris cleared her throat and wiped her mouth with the napkin. "That was delicious, Amy. You must give me your recipe. I've never had pan-fried chicken fried steak before. I do believe it's far better than deep-fried." She patted her stomach to show just how much she enjoyed the meal.

Pleased, Amy piped in, "The secret is in the skillet, Doris. My cast-iron skillet has been passed down from my great grandmother to her daughter, and so on. That's a lot of family love that goes into every meal. This may sound silly, but I think everything tastes better when it's cooked in that skillet."

"It's not silly at all, sweetheart. It's beautiful. There's *nothing* more important than family. I think I'll go out and get a cast iron skillet myself. That's a tradition I'd like to start. The meal was lovely, and the pie, well, the pie was to die for," Doris said and then looked out over the table to the rest of the people. "I should probably get back to the girls. I'm sure they're going stir crazy in the hotel room." Doris slid her chair out and motioned to Bright Flower. "Why don't you walk me out, child? I want to get to know you a little better." Everyone seated at the table momentarily froze and glanced at Doris. Their gazes shifted to Bright Flower in unison.

Smiling, she nodded and stood. Nathan got to his feet, but Doris shut him down. "You sit down, son. We'll be fine."

Bright Flower nodded to Nathan, letting him know she had this situation under control. "Do as your mother said, Nathan. I'll be back in a bit."

Doris slid her purse on her shoulder and hooked arms with Bright Flower. "You have the most beautiful name. How did you get it?"

She's behaving, so I'll reciprocate. Patting the woman's hand on her arm, Bright Flower relayed one of her people's customs. "My grandfather gave it to me. Names are important in my culture. There is even a naming ritual performed. Nature is the guiding force behind choosing the right name. On the day I was born, a field of Indian Paintbrush wildflowers bloomed outside of our home. Grandfather believed the Creator had blessed my family by the offering and thereby chose my name. The flower has had great significance in my life. Every time I come across an unexpected bloom, I know that something good is about to happen." She offered a genuine smile to Nathan's mother. "This is not the season for blooms. Yesterday, the Creator gave me the gift of an Indian Paintbrush at the base of our stairs. It was a good omen of things to come. Today, Nathan and I wed."

Doris stopped in her tracks and clutched Bright Flower's arm tighter. "Oh my. That's a beautiful story."

Nathan's mother then gently cupped Bright Flower's cheeks between her hands and said, "I'm sorry if I was rude before. Truthfully, I was more than a little stunned to learn that my son had married without telling me. It's not an adequate excuse, but he's my son. I worry about him."

"I understand. I'm sorry too. I wish we could have waited, but my people do things differently."

Doris offered a smile. "I look forward to getting to know you. You look at my son with such love and devotion, how could I not accept you into our family?" Tears gently rolled down the woman's cheeks as she patted her chest. "Oh dear, and the way my Nathan looks at you…" Doris gushed "…that look reminds me of his dear father. Oh, child, I wish you could've met him. He was a beautiful soul. Just like my sweet son."

The door creaked, breaking into the moment. Nathan joined the women on the front porch. Doris brushed a kiss on Bright Flower's cheek and then hugged Nathan. "Goodnight, son." The woman turned and hurried off to her car without another word.

Nathan placed his arm across Bright Flower's shoulders. "It looks like my mom may be coming around. She didn't say anything to upset you, did she?"

Squeezing his waist, Bright Flower lifted her face and smiled up at him. "Of course not. Your mother is observant. She was pleased with the way I look at you."

Nathan grinned and bent to kiss her lips. "I'm partial to that myself."

****

By the time Nathan and Bright Flower made it back inside the cabin, everyone had moved from the dining room to the great room. A fire blazed in the fireplace. Nathan noticed Mac had disappeared. He'd probably taken shelter upstairs.

Jody approached them and offered hugs all around. "That couldn't have been easy." Grabbing Bright Flower's hands, she said, "I've known Doris my whole life. She's been a second mother to me. She can be gruff, especially when it comes to Nathan, but she would do anything if it meant he was happy. Give her some time. She'll come around.

"I've got some champagne chilling for you, and we moved Jursic's stuff from the guest house." Jody reached up and tweaked Nathan's nose. "I love you, and I'm so extremely happy for you. Terry's got a big day ahead tomorrow." She sent an elbow into Nathan's stomach. "He's the last of us three musketeers to tie the knot." Jody reached out and hugged Bright Flower. "We all got so lucky. We found our better halves."

****

Another hour passed when Nathan feigned a yawn. *I'm going to go stir crazy if I have to wait much longer to get Bright Flower alone.*

Nathan's cell phone dinged. Pulling it from his pocket, he read the text message and grinned. He turned the phone so Bright Flower could see the note. "It looks like my mom has calmed down. This message is from my sister."

WTF dude?!?!? Mom would've gone ballistic if I would've gotten married without her knowing. She's already completed a to-do list for your formal wedding. Now she's pacing the floor saying something about the importance of naming a child. She's eating chocolate-covered peanuts and spewing all kinds of bizarre names like Great Peanut and Cluster of Love for her 'hopefully' soon-to-be grandbabies. She mentioned something about Navajo tradition. I didn't know they appreciated a chocolate peanut cluster the way mom does. You always were her favorite.

Bright Flower's blush warmed his heart. The urgency to get her alone became critical.

Chapter Fourteen

There was a slight foggy mist forming in the forest surrounding the trail. The damp haze cocooned Bright Flower and the man she loved, lending a dream-like quality to their stroll. *Thank you, Creator, for giving this man to me.* She allowed a wide grin to blossom. *It took you long enough to deliver him.*

The cool Flagstaff evening was chilly but did nothing to tamp the smoldering need Bright Flower had suppressed for far too long. Holding hands the two of them ambled at a leisurely pace down the winding path enjoying their first moments alone as husband and wife. When she shivered, Nathan tucked her into his side. "Are you cold, sweetheart? Let me carry the champagne."

She couldn't stop smiling. Handing the bottle off, Bright Flower wrapped her arms around his waist and squeezed. "No. I'm not cold at all. I'm happy and excited. I love you, Nathan." He squeezed her tighter under the crook of his arm and bent to kiss the top of her head. "I love you too, Bright Flower. I can't believe this is real."

The cabin came into view as they rounded the curve on the path. Tucked into a stand of Ponderosa Pine, the house and surrounding trees glowed with soft outdoor lights. It was lovely. Bright Flower couldn't have picked a better place to spend her wedding night.

The soft radiance of a blaze in the fireplace flickered through the front picture window inviting them to enter. Nathan chuckled. "As if you couldn't tell Jody's a romantic at heart. If I know that woman, she's left more surprises for us inside."

Nathan set the champagne and flutes down on a table outside the front door and turned to face Bright Flower. There was something on his mind that had him worrying his cheek with his teeth.

Since there was such a disparity in the height, Bright Flower tugged on Nathan's shirt to bring him closer. Placing her hand on the side of his face, she gazed into his eyes. "Are you not happy? What has you so worried that you'd bite your lip?"

Nathan's hands cradled her face, and Bright Flower wondered how someone so large could be so gentle. Her eyes shut, and the corner of her lips curved up. She basked in his tenderness while waiting for him to reply. "I've been dreaming about this moment for so long. I want this to be perfect for you. I know that you've never been with a man."

Not wanting him to see how nervous she was, Bright Flower buried her face into his chest. If she was honest, she'd have to admit that she was frightened but probably not for the reasons he thought. Her mother had died years ago. She'd been far too young to be schooled in the art of lovemaking. Her biggest fear was disappointing him. "You are my husband. I love you. You are perfect in every way. It's just that…" His heart was pounding against her cheek.

"Yes?"

"Well, I don't know what I'm doing. Will you tell

me if I do something wrong?" The rhythm of his breathing all but stopped. *Oh no! I've already upset him.*

Nathan nudged Bright Flower back a step. His expression was tender. Gently grabbing her by the shoulders, he bent down and touched his nose to hers. "You are my wife. I am your husband. There is *nothing* in this world that you could say or do that would disappoint me. Think of it this way. We will teach each other. You do what feels right to you. I'll do what feels right to me. If we don't like something, we'll tell each other. You are free to explore. Free to be yourself. It's important to me to meet all of your wants and needs. We are one now, so there is no reason for any doubt. Ever."

Unable to look Nathan in the eye, she fumbled with the buttons on his shirt. "You want me to be myself?"

After a moment of silence, Bright Flower felt his fingers under her chin, gently lifting her face. "Of course, I do. Why would you doubt that?"

She wanted to look away, but Nathan refused to let her budge. "Throughout the years, Grandfather insisted that I portray myself as submissive in public. He believed that doing so reflected a woman's nurturing side and provided a show of respect for others. He told me more times than I can count that men did not want or value a woman with opinions or a temper. Considering the importance of our roles in the community, and how our tribesmen and women look up to us, it was imperative to be the perfect model for all young Navajo girls. Never before have I dared to show my true self to anyone but Grandfather."

In one fell swoop, Nathan lifted Bright Flower off

the ground and kissed her hard. The yearning for this man had been building her entire life—even though, those outside her culture might think she'd lost her mind for marrying a man she'd only met once before being wed, she didn't care. Her husband, whom she loved beyond reason, gave her the power to free herself. She vowed to heed his words and come out of her shell. She could do it for him. She *would* do it for him. The time had come to express her love for this man, and she intended to put her thoughts into action.

Nathan's mouth found her neck. His lips searched out her pulse. She was sure he'd feel the swiftness of her racing heart rate beneath his lips. Need clenched at Bright Flower's core sending her into a frenzy. Her legs wrapped around his waist which only increased the agonizing burn within her. Although she might not know exactly what she wanted, or how to express her need, she did know that she wanted it all. Opening the door, Nathan carried her over the threshold and gently placed her on the couch. She couldn't wait to see what he did next.

Kneeling between her legs, he peered deep into her eyes. Her husband didn't make a sound, but his nostrils flared as he looked his fill. Hoping to encourage him, Bright Flower licked her lips. Her eyelids felt weighted down, and she allowed them to close. Using her knees, she guided Nathan closer. Breathless with want, she whispered, "My heart is beating so fast. I don't think I can wait, Nathan, I want you. I've waited so long to be with you like this, to feel every touch and kiss. Show me. Teach me."

Nathan's finger lightly traced her face as if he were memorizing every detail. He found the scar on the side of her chin and bent to caress it with his lips. Her breath hitched as his perfect mouth moved tenderly down her throat. Unbuttoning her shirt, he slid the blouse from her shoulders. A moment of embarrassment hit her as she realized she wore a basic bra, nothing exciting. Bright Flower silently cursed her grandfather for not telling her of his plans. If she'd known this morning where the day would lead, she would have dressed for the occasion. She carefully scrutinized Nathan's reaction and was relieved to find that even with the ugly underwear, his expression hid nothing. He wanted her.

The image of that sultry visage empowered Bright Flower and would be forever ingrained in her mind. Her husband's lust made her feel desirable and loved as a woman for the first time in her life. She'd never felt so strong, so needed before. Leaning her head back on the couch, she watched her partner's every reaction through half-closed eyelids. Enjoying this new role, she decided to take the buffalo by the horns.

Bright Flower stretched her back and leaned forward so she could unhook the bra. Her husband groaned and spurred her on. Teasing Nathan with her body was her new favorite thing. Biting her lip, she nudged a strap off of one shoulder. His body vibrated between her locked knees sending twitches of pleasure from her bellybutton straight down to her nether region.

A groan escaped Nathan's lips as he pushed the straps down farther. His fingers grazed the top of her full breasts. Bright Flower's body arched and swayed on its own accord. There was no thinking. No planning. Just feeling.

Her breasts fell free, the nipples erect and aching for his attention. A glorious moan, one of pure pleasure, erupted from her throat as Nathan cupped her breasts and squeezed her nipples. The sound of this man enjoying her body produced stirrings of passion that quivered through every cell of her being. Bright Flower's legs tightened around him as she ground her center into his rock-hard abdomen. Nathan's tongue started the journey from her bellybutton to her breasts, and she thought she'd go mad. Slowly he teased the underside of her breasts. Bright Flower's body seemed to have a mind of its own as she gave in to these powerful new sensations. Writhing, she brazenly screamed his name in between pants for air.

Cupping her breasts, Bright Flower offered the hardened tips to her partner. Nathan surprised her when he took one of them with his teeth, nipping, and suckling until she cried out. All awkwardness relinquished, her hands frantically pulled at his clothes, but he wasn't ready to release her just yet. Placing his hand between their bodies, Nathan gained access to her jeans. After sliding the zipper, he tugged her britches and panties down as far as he could without losing contact.

Nathan suddenly pulled away. His eyes made a slow journey over her body. He seemed to enjoy looking at her. But his absence caused Bright Flower's lips to pout with disappointment. Missing his touch, she pinched her nipples, and whispered, "Don't stop, please don't stop." Realizing her actions had the desired effect, she grinned wickedly. His jaw tensed, and those beautiful brown eyes turned almost black as they burned with desire while she caressed herself.

Nathan uttered the sexiest whimper she'd ever heard. The sound provided another clue as to just how much he was enjoying himself. Frantically Nathan broke her leg lock. Yanking the jeans and underwear from her feet, he tossed the pants across the room. Bright Flower felt powerful as she openly displayed her womanhood. When he licked his lips, something deep inside her shifted. Unseen sparks deep within her core sent a powerful shudder throughout her body.

Enjoying this new seductress role, Bright Flower brazenly slid her hand down her belly. Her pleasure nodule throbbed almost painfully. The skimming sensation jarred a spasm that ran so deep, she thought her soul had fractured. Crying out, she couldn't catch her breath. Before the last tremor had ceased, Nathan had undressed and knelt between her legs. Nathan's strong hands gripped her thighs as he ran his thumbs through Bright Flower's slit sending more earth-shattering jolts through her system. Exquisite pleasure ripped through her core, and all cognitive thought was lost.

"Was that your first orgasm?" Pride rang loud and clear in Nathan's voice.

Bright Flower had lost the capability to speak. She couldn't think. Shoot, she couldn't breathe.

Chuckling Nathan lifted her feet to his shoulders. "Let's see how long it takes to get you to number two. Shall we?"

Nathan slid his tongue throughout the length of her womanhood. Bright Flower yanked his hair and ground herself into his mouth. Latching onto her nub, he swirled, and everything went dark. Stars filled the inside of her eyelids as her body spasmed and shook. Panting was the only way to fuel her oxygen-starved lungs. His finger slid inside with ease and her body constricted around his digit. Somewhere off in the distance she heard his teasing question. "Are you ready for number three?"

Watching his wife's reactions to his ministrations staggered Nathan. *I'm a lucky man.* Not only was Bright Flower receptive to his lovemaking, but she'd also successfully cast off the submissive role which had been drummed into her psyche for decades. His woman had turned into a firestorm of passion, and he couldn't be prouder.

Kissing her thigh, Nathan worried about how small and tight Bright Flower was. He didn't have any experience with virgins. Concern over hurting her was growing with each minute that passed. He wanted the first time to be special, something she'd remember for the rest of her life. The thought of causing her pain had gnawed at him since they started the moonlit walk to the guest house.

The pressure of Bright Flower's feet on his shoulders suddenly shifted and grew stronger until she'd pushed him on his back. She sprang up from the couch and stood over Nathan—beautiful, sensual, and seductive. His Indian princess scanned every inch of his body. Her eyes landed on the length of him, and she grinned. His bride was an innocent when it came to lovemaking, but she was learning fast. Under her scrutiny, his erection jumped. Pivoting, she offered a full view of her backside while straddling him. Once on her hands and knees, she shook her ass in his face, offering herself to him while licking the line of hair down his belly leading to his painful rock-hard erection.

"I'm ready for number three now, husband."

His pleasure produced a groan from deep in his

belly as his fingers parted her. He gently nipped the swollen nub as her cheek brushed against his erection. Thrusting his pelvis up, he offered himself, hoping against hope that she'd take him in her mouth. She did one better. She licked the length of him as if he were a lollipop. Everything ceased except for what that luscious mouth was doing to him. Her tongue swirled around the head, and he shuddered in delight. Her lips parted for him, and he pumped into her mouth. His balls were so tight that he thought he'd explode. She reached around his leg and grabbed his sac. *Oh my God! I have to stop this or I'm...*

Before he could move, she broke her hold on him and stood. This time when Bright Flower turned to face Nathan, she knelt down and straddled him, cradling the head of his erection at the edge of her woman's sheath. She slid the tip of him to her nub and shuddered. A serene expression crossed her face. "I love you," he whispered in awe.

His beautiful wife's eyes opened a slit, and she offered him a smile. "We were chosen by the Creator. We are meant for each other and fit together in every way." Her expression was one of sheer bliss. Raising herself and pinning him in her gaze, she fisted his erection and guided him inside her.

Inch by precious inch Bright Flower's body molded to his. She shuddered and started to rock her hips. With him buried so deeply inside her body, each magnificent move of their lovemaking brought Nathan closer to climax. Reaching down, he tickled her nub. Her orgasm spawned a moment of sheer electricity between them. Grabbing her hips, he thrust one final time before following his bride over the edge.

Bright Flower collapsed on top of him. After a few moments of heavy breathing she giggled and raised a flushed face to his. Kissing the bottom of his chin, she grinned. Her fingers anxiously strummed his chest. "That was fun! Let's do it again."

Chapter Fifteen

Nathan was disappointed with how fast their alone time sped by. But wasn't that always the case with joyous occasions? Long before he or Bright Flower wanted, they joined the others for his best friend's wedding. Spirit Keeper had bowed out of the festivities claiming there were too many essential issues needing his attention in preparation for the battle ahead.

It had been a stellar day of celebration. Rainy and Terry's mid-day wedding and the reception was winding down. Nathan finally had the opportunity to twirl the bride around the dance floor.

Terry's bride had surprised everyone when she appeared for her special day with vibrant streaks of purple and pink in her auburn locks. The colorful tresses trailed down her shoulder in a fancy curled ponytail. While Nathan was a simple man and had always preferred the natural look, he had to admit that his best friend's new wife was stunning even with multihued hair.

The bride's dress was a soft shade of honey. The gauzy material seemed to somehow float on the air giving her the appearance of an angel in motion. Like Rainy's fairytale hair, the bottom of the gown sported streaks of color, one fading into the other. From the softest hue of pink to a striking shade of purple, the dress personified nature and the most glorious aspects of a rainbow. He'd wondered what type of wedding gown would befit a Wiccan High Priestess and wasn't disappointed with her choice. Rainy was the epitome of every artist's dream, and with her standing by his side, his best friend had beamed all morning. He could only imagine the beautiful portrait Terry would create from this memorable day.

"I will love you the rest of my life for putting that goofy grin on Terry's face. You're one of our circle now, Rainy. Jody brought Jared in. Terry brought you in." He paused, searching for his new bride but didn't see her. "And I brought Bright Flower.

"We've grown from three to six. I'll grant you that we're an odd bunch, but we're family now. If there's anything you ever need, we'll all come running. It's what we've always done for each other."

Rainy stopped and slugged him in the shoulder. "Dammit it, Nathan. You made me cry again. My makeup can't take much more of this."

With his head thrown back, Nathan released a hearty laugh. All morning the tension of Mac's land problems and the immensity of what faced them tomorrow had weighed Nathan down. It felt good to let loose and forget about all of their problems for a bit. How could he be anxious when Bright Flower had been by his side all day? With time growing short, Nathan pulled the bride back into his arms and swung her around until her feet left the ground. She chortled with glee and squeezed him tighter.

Nathan thought of Terry dancing with Bright Flower earlier. Something warmed deep in his heart when he saw two of the most important people in his life enjoying themselves together. Up until this point his mother had completely monopolized his new bride's time. He could only imagine what they'd discussed.

Scanning the few remaining guests, Nathan inquired of the bride, "Have you seen Mac? I wanted to touch base with him before Bright Flower and I left for Spirit Keeper's camp."

Rainy responded, "I haven't seen him in a while. I'm sorry to say that he looked uncomfortable. I'm pretty sure he slipped out right after the ceremony."

Nathan nodded his understanding. "I feel bad for the guy. He's struggling with the supernatural aspects of the land issues. Who could blame him? You've got to give him credit though. Lacking any other explanation, he seems to have accepted the problem for what it is—at least for the moment.

"Mac has to be worried that his Arizona ranch might never get off of the ground. The man would suffer an expensive setback if the issues aren't resolved. He seems to be the sort of person that would always err on the side of caution. Being honorable, I feel confident that he would never purposely jeopardize anyone's life, human or animal. That means the ranch will probably remain abandoned if we fail.

"That puts a lot of pressure on my shoulders. I feel like I have to get this right for him. I can't share much about his private life and what he's been through over the last year, but Mac's had a grim time. He deserves a good break."

A deafening crash of glass breaking from just outside the wedding tent startled everyone. A blood-curdling scream followed close behind. "Jared! Nathan! Help!" Shock and terror echoed in the frantic shriek.

Rainy's hand flew to her mouth. "Nathan, that's Cheryl screaming!"

He immediately canvassed the wedding tent to check on his bride—still no sign of her. Jared was already running for the entryway. Nathan sprinted across the dance floor and got to the entrance just as the curtain yanked open. Cheryl, carrying Amy's son in a tight grasp, ran straight into Nathan and Jared's arms. "It's…" She panted, trying to get enough air to speak. "It's Amy. A man attacked her in the house. Hurry! He has a knife. Bright Flower is trying to fight him off."

Time slowed to a snail's pace. His thumping heartbeat dulled all external sound. Nathan didn't think—he didn't weigh his options. Bright Flower was in trouble, and he'd kill any man who would dare put a hand on her. Nathan took the stairs three at a time with Jared close on his heels. He burst through the door and got the fright of his life.

Bright Flower was on her back. A man straddled her body—a knife held above her chest. "Say please! I want to hear you beg for your life."

Nathan propelled himself forward, but Jared caught him. He fought against his friend's hold. "No! Think, Nathan. If you hit him, the momentum could push the knife into Bright Flower. I'll grab his right arm, and you take his left," his friend ordered. "We'll yank him off of her together. It's the safest way."

Bright Flower screamed something in Navajo as her knee slammed into the man's groin. Her forehead connected with the offender's face, and his knife went flying. Having the upper hand, she pushed off with her leg and rolled both of their bodies across the floor. It only took a split second for her to yank a hidden dagger from her boot and press it against the man's throat. "Say, please," she hissed.

Nathan yanked her off of the assailant and landed a sound punch to his face. The sound and feel of bone and cartilage breaking gave him immense pleasure. The action was enough to knock the attacker out cold.

Mac ran through the front door of the house brandishing a large metal pipe as a makeshift weapon. "I heard screams," the rancher yelled. Bright Flower was on the floor trying to comfort Amy. That's when Nathan noticed the blood.

He pulled his wife off of the floor. Placing her feet first on the ground in front of him, he patted Bright Flower's body frantically examining her for injuries. "Are you cut? Where is the blood coming from?"

Bright Flower clutched his hands. "It's not me. Amy's been hurt." She released him and grabbed a pillow off of the couch to place under Amy's head. Nathan's brain was spinning. Mac shoved him out of the way and put pressure on an oozing knife wound Amy had sustained on her arm. Nathan grabbed his knees to catch his breath.

Jared called out, "The police and ambulance are on their way. How bad is Amy hurt, Mac?" When Nathan didn't hear a response, he glanced at the cowboy. He was white as a ghost. The man took a deep breath and said, "The arm wound looks pretty serious. I'll keep the pressure on it."

Bright Flower chimed in. "It looks like her ankle is broken too. She's got a nasty bump on her head, but her eyes are focused. I don't want to move her, so beyond that, I couldn't tell you."

Nathan watched the rancher gently stroke Amy's

hair. He bent down and cooed, "Everything's all right, Amy. I've got you." She placed a shaky hand over Mac's and cried, "My boy…Is Marcus okay? Please, I need my boy."

Not wanting to crowd her, Nathan stayed where he was and stated calmly, "Cheryl has Marcus. He's doing just fine. Who is this man that attacked you, Amy? Do you know him?"

She slammed her eyes shut and wailed. It was a horrible sound that squeezed at Nathan's heart. Mac put his face close to hers and whispered something only meant for her to hear. Whatever he said had worked. She took a deep breath, relaxed the muscles in her face, and stared into Mac's eyes. "That's right. You just keep looking at me, little darlin'. I've got you. Now, do you know who that man is?"

"Marc's dad sent him. The last thing he said to me before he hurt me was, '*This is from your husband.*' "

Mac offered a smirk to the injured woman. "Well, that wasn't very smart of him now, was it?" Nathan couldn't believe what he was seeing. Savagely beaten and cut, Amy peered into Mac's eyes and smiled.

Chapter Sixteen

There was still quite a bit of light left when Nathan and Bright Flower arrived at Spirit Keeper's camp. Before exiting the vehicle, Nathan grabbed her hand and squeezed. "What happened to everyone? There are only two tents left."

Bright Flower kissed the back of his hand and replied, "It would not be appropriate for them to stay. We have important business to discuss and only a short period of time. You must be trained in our ways." Her brow furrowed as she looked away. When Bright Flower turned back to Nathan, she was biting her lip. "Spirit Keeper will insist that we stay here tonight."

"Okay. But what's wrong?"

"I'm worried. I believe there are things my grandfather wants you to do that you shouldn't. They could bring you harm. I will not allow that to happen."

Warmth bathed his body as she promised to protect him. Leaning over he kissed her. "I love you too."

A large bonfire blazed. After greeting Spirit Keeper, Bright Flower forced herself between them and occupied the space directly to the old man's left. Nathan knew precisely what she was doing and couldn't help but chuckle. By ensuring Nathan sat as far away from her grandfather as possible, his lovely wife was using herself as a buffer. If necessary, she was his first line of defense. Against what? He had no clue.

The old man appeared to be deep in thought. Spirit Keeper's hand rested on a huge and scarred leather bag situated on a bale of hay to his right. The tote was so large that it must have taken several animal skins to create. Wondering what secrets lay within that ancient duffle Nathan sat quietly, gazing into the flames. He'd promised himself to be open to whatever his new grandfather presented. What other option did he have?

Minutes passed by as Spirit Keeper's reflections remained internal. Nathan emptied his mind and focused on the blaze. He closed his eyes and breathed in the deep, rich scent of burning oak. There was something primal about the smell of smoldering wood that relaxed Nathan and offered a sense of peace which allowed his anxiety to melt away.

Thwack. Nathan almost jumped out of his skin. Spirit Keeper had slapped the fire with a heavy tree limb sending sparks flying everywhere. "We are up against evil. You are not familiar with the ways of my people. You must learn fast to trust your heart and believe that we can succeed."

Spirit Keeper opened the flap of the supple doeskin bag and searched through the contents. He produced a simple old-fashioned bow that looked as if it belonged in a museum. With shuttered eyes, his grandfather by marriage raised the weapon to the sky and spoke to the heavens in his native tongue. Lowering the bow, he lovingly caressed it before holding the weapon out to Nathan.

Nathan stretched and reached out for the bow, but before he could grasp the weapon, Bright Flower stood and vehemently objected. "Grandfather. No!" The force of her protest prompted Nathan to jerk his hand back. "That is a ceremonial bow made from wood struck with lightning. *You* know as well as *I* do that my husband must not touch that. He will become ill."

Spirit Keeper's eyes squinted, and his gaze zeroed in on his granddaughter. Clearly unhappy with the outburst the old man's jaw tightened as he slammed the weapon onto his lap. "Enough, Granddaughter! Sit." Even though outrage boomed in his voice, Bright Flower stood her ground. Crossing her arms in defiance, she scooted farther to her left and stood fearlessly in front of Nathan.

After a few tense moments, Spirit Keeper released a heavy sigh. His demeanor softened. "This man is my grandson. It makes no difference that he was not born to our people. The Creator chose him for you. He has spoken to me through a dream quest. Nathan will fight the evil, not as a white man but as one of us." A loud thump sounded as his fist slammed into his chest. "Nathan has the heart of a Navajo—the heart of a warrior—the heart of a singer. He will not be denied the tools of such because his wife fears for him. Now sit back down and do not interrupt again. We have much to discuss."

Bright Flower continued to stand defiantly. Nathan rose behind his fierce wife and placed his large hands on her shoulders to offer comfort. Kissing the top of her head, he smiled to Spirit Keeper. "You have raised a firebrand, sir. Bright Flower is not afraid to speak her mind for those she loves. I am proud to call her my wife. You should be proud as well." He turned Bright Flower around and cupped her face. "Spirit Keeper believes that I can help. He is family now. I trust him.

Sit down and let's listen to what he has to say." Her answer was clear as day in her eyes. She didn't want to listen. "Let's just hear what he has to say," Nathan reinforced his words. His bride finally acquiesced and allowed him to guide her back to her seat.

As if the bow gave Spirit Keeper strength, the old man held tight to the weapon while his determined gaze captured Nathan's attention. "Your mind may find that my teachings are unbelievable. You must open your heart to all that I say and know that through the Creator's power *all* is possible. Without your belief, we will fail." Once again, he held the bow out. Bright Flower's breath hitched when Nathan reached forward and grabbed the weapon before any further objections could be made.

Trying to get a feel for this antique armament, Nathan stroked the blemished bow and examined every inch. Streaks of burnt and bruised wood scarred the weapon's surface. He marveled at the elegance of the simple hieroglyphic carvings covering the surface. He'd never seen the bow's equal. "It's beautiful." He hesitated. This relic belonged in a museum, *not* in a close-quarter fight. His chest tightened as apprehension took root. "It's apparent that this is a special bow, sir. Am I missing something? This weapon doesn't appear to be meant for battle but instead should be used as a ceremonial piece. Please forgive me if my question seems out of line. But are you expecting us to defeat your brother *and* the spirit skinwalkers using only this?" He lifted the bow. "I can't wrap my head around crushing such an enemy with nothing more than an antiquated weapon."

Spirit Keeper smiled, seemingly pleased with

Nathan's queries. "You are correct, Grandson. This bow is special and has been used in many ceremonies. The Creator himself provided the materials for this weapon. It has special properties and is our only way to fight the evil that we face effectively. Let me ask you this—is there any *modern* weapon that would dispatch many angry spirits in one fell swoop? Think back to that night when the evil ones trapped you in their clutches. I used this very weapon to fend them off."

Feeling silly, Nathan nodded. "You have a point."

"This weapon is a gift from the Creator and carries his powerful energy. The holy one reached out with his own hand and touched this wood. Only singers can handle this anointed weapon. *All* others that dare defy this tenet are doomed to illness. Death may even touch them.

"When spirits living outside of the Underworld are branded by the sacred arrows, their souls become dust never to see the light of day again. Nothing evil can survive the Holy One's power."

Nathan's eyebrows rose. "I don't mean any disrespect but if that's the case, couldn't you just shoot your brother with this bow and arrow? Wouldn't that kill him and remove the threat?"

Spirit Keeper's lips were pursed so tightly Nathan regretted asking the question. "He is a living being and has not yet crossed into spirit form. His power far exceeds that of his followers. There is only one way to stop him, but now is not the time to discuss that. The task of my brother's death is for me to fulfill.

"Now, come. We will see how well you shoot."

Nathan stood and started to follow Spirit Keeper. "I'm afraid I haven't shot a bow and arrow since I was a kid and *that* was just a toy."

They stood in the middle of a meadow facing a large rock with cans scattered across the top. The light was fading fast making the targets almost invisible. Spirit Keeper handed Nathan an arrow and showed him how to load the bow. "Before you pull the bowstring back, close your eyes. Imagine your enemy before you. Feel the Creator's power. Know in your heart that you cannot miss. The Creator will guide the arrow to its intended mark."

Oh boy.

Bright Flower touched his arm and smiled up at him. "The Holy One has spoken. You can do this."

Nathan closed his eyes, pictured the cans off in the distance, and prayed this worked. Ready or not he opened his eyes and gave the targeted soda can his full attention. There was a hushed whoosh as he pulled the bowstring back. A deep, calming breath helped him relax his fingers as Nathan released the string. *Twang.* The arrow had misfired and landed at his feet. *Shit.*

He shot four arrows, each one gaining a little distance from the last. His best shot was only twenty feet in front of him. Spirit Keeper sighed. "Let's go back to the fire and talk."

Bright Flower added some wood as Spirit Keeper sat beside Nathan and glared into the blaze. It was apparent the old man was trying to come to some sort of decision. "While I believe that you trust me and all that I say, growing up as a white man has blinded your mind to our ways. You may find it difficult to open yourself to your new role and a Navajo singer's gifts."

"Sir, I mean no disrespect, but these ideas are all new to me. I really want to be who you think I am—and

I'm trying my best—but I have no clue what I'm doing."

Spirit Keeper nodded. "All will come when you release your reservations about our ways. We must first drink a potion to free your mind. The potent liquid will cease your fears and allow all barriers to fall. Are you willing?"

Nathan hesitated. "A potion?"

"I would not give you anything that would harm you. Do you trust me to open your mind to the Creator's ways?"

Nathan glanced at Bright Flower for insight. Her lips were pressed together so tightly it was easy to see her reservations without her speaking a word. *She's worried, but since she's not stepping in, this potion must be safe. At this point, it's go all in or go home.*

"Yes." He hesitated, wondering if he should inquire more about the potion before proceeding. Nathan made eye contact with Spirit Keeper and found strength in his gaze. "Okay. I trust you."

His wife released a deep exhale and lowered her shoulders as if defeated.

"Granddaughter, please prepare the drink for my grandson and me." After a slight hesitation, Bright Flower opened a leather satchel and removed an empty earthen bowl along with a jar filled to the brim with a dark, cloudy concoction. She started to chant. Pouring the liquid into the handmade vessel, she then used tongs to drop a hot coal from the fire into the liquid. Fascinated, Nathan watched as his wife closed her eyes and continued to chant while swirling the mixture.

The concoction was passed to Spirit Keeper. He drank the contents and handed the empty bowl back to

Bright Flower. Performing the same steps, she filled the vessel again, dropped an ember into the mixture, and offered the potion to Nathan. When he hesitated, Spirit Keeper spoke up, "Drink. Doing so will prove your trust in our ways. This tonic will open your mind and remove any fear and barriers to our teachings."

The liquid tasted foul, but Nathan managed to gulp down the entire contents of the bowl. The concoction burned as it churned its way into his stomach. The inside of his mouth started to water, and he prayed he would keep the nasty liquid down.

Bright Flower returned to Nathan's side, but remained quiet. Spirit Keeper sat with a small, animal-skin drum tucked onto his lap. Grasping an antler with the gnarled hands that came with advanced age, the old man raised his arm over his head. He swung down and hit the drum once. Grandfather tilted his head back as he cried out into the darkening sky in his native language.

Spirit Keeper rhythmically hit the drum and continued to chant. Nathan relaxed and allowed himself to focus on each strike of the antler. The percussive beat started to overwhelm his senses. Everything around him faded to dark. All he could feel was the constant drumbeat resonating deep inside him.

Each cell in Nathan's body seemed to respond and vibrate to the beat. His ears started to falter and felt plugged as if he were in a vacuum. A tingling sensation ran the course of his body from the crown of his head to the tips of his toes.

Nathan glanced past the fire and into the growing shadows of the pines. Orbs of light—some white, some gold—danced between the branches like the soap bubbles he used to blow as a kid. They gathered and formed a large circle around the area. Far off in the distance, Nathan could hear disembodied voices joining in Spirit Keeper's chant.

Something substantial nudged Nathan's arm. When he turned his upper body to see what this new interruption was, the world spun for a moment. Trying not to blackout he threw his hands up to brace his spinning head. A buffalo grunted and snorted with pleasure beside him. Childlike delight struck him hard as Nathan raised his hand and touched the beast he'd become so familiar with in his dreams. "My spirit animal."

Unsure whether he'd spoken aloud or not, the buffalo greeted him with a nudge to his cheek and grunted as if he'd been heard. The animal took its place next to Nathan. A raptor's cry screeched through the night as Bright Flower's eagle landed on top of the bison's massive head.

Beside him, Bright Flower started to sing a haunting chant, but she sounded miles away. The fire popped before Nathan and directed his attention forward. The distant light orbs began to twinkle and change shape. Before he knew what was happening, glowing Native Americans danced around them—some were women, some children, but most were men. Their expressions appeared loving and hopeful.

With each turn around the fire, the specter Indians moved closer. Nathan jumped when he felt a forceful tap on his back. A beautiful Indian woman bent and placed her hand on his shoulder. Instinctively Nathan knew that she was offering a piece of herself for the struggle ahead. They were all there to support the effort to clear the land of evil and save as many of the souls damned by a madman as possible. He should be frightened, but the generosity of shared strength and sense of complete belonging was oddly touching instead. He would accept what was given and use it wholeheartedly.

Nathan tried to stand but couldn't seem to control his body. His legs felt like rubber, and his equilibrium was shattered—leaving him staggered by vertigo. The buffalo offered its head for stability, and he was able to get to his feet. Bright Flower's eagle shrieked a cry of encouragement and came closer to nuzzle his hair.

Spirit Keeper grabbed Nathan's arm and guided him back to the now pitch-black meadow. Grandfather stood with his back to the cans and said, "Watch and learn."

Facing the wrong direction, the old man pointed the ceremonial bow and fired. The arrow illuminated the sky like a crackling rod of lightning and left a trail of brilliant light in its wake. The projectile curved and shifted one-hundred and eighty degrees in mid-air and shot straight over their heads zeroing in on the cans. Before the arrow reached its mark, one of the pop cans—Nathan assumed it was the intended target— burst into flames and fell to the ground. A slight rumble of thunder sounded in the distance under a clear night's sky.

Spirit Keeper offered the weapon to Nathan, and he accepted. Raw power surged beneath his fingers. The bow pulsed in his grasp as if it were a living breathing entity.

The cans on the rock were now completely hidden deep within the darkness of night, but he pointed in the general direction. Before Nathan released the arrow, an intense force swelled and swirled within his gut. The power came from everything surrounding him—nature, ghosts of those he'd seen earlier, and the woman he loved beyond measure. The urge to throw his head back and shout won over. The war cry started deep in his belly. Every emotion—love, hate, fear—built into one powerful surge and lashed out from his body like thunder.

The arrow flew. Lightning again sparked in the sky. As if drawn to the arrow, the brilliant bolt of electricity converged on the flying projectile. The meadow lit up, and the boulder holding the cans exploded. Heaven above applauded Nathan's efforts with a loud rumbling thunderclap.

His buffalo danced around and stopped face to face with Nathan. The animal seemed to be smiling as Nathan lovingly cradled the beast's head. "We did it, boy."

Chapter Seventeen

Nathan could smell the bacon and fresh-baked biscuits from outside. His mouth watered, but his stomach was boiling. He rapped on the back door and let himself in. Everyone, except Jody and Terry, sat stone-faced around the kitchen table. They were busy at the stove, preparing a breakfast feast. The mood seemed somber. He was almost afraid to ask, "What's the news on Amy?"

Jody crossed the room, and he bent down so she could give him a peck on the cheek. "Sit down. You look a little green this morning. I'll get you a cup of coffee."

Terry set a heaping plate of bacon and a sky-high stack of biscuits on the table.

Nathan rubbed his belly and decided dumping hot coffee into it might not be the best thing. He promised himself he wouldn't even look at the bacon. "Thanks, but no coffee for me. Tell me about Amy."

Jody paused, and tears welled in her eyes. She blinked fast to keep them at bay. "Well, she needed a lot of stitches to patch up her arm, and her ankle is broken. They didn't want to operate on her last night because her poor little body had been through too much trauma as it was. Oh, Nathan, that man really hurt her. She's bruised from head to toe. They're going to hold off on surgery until tomorrow. The doctors think she'll be in a better frame of mind by then." She waved a spatula in the direction of the rancher. "Amy was so scared, that Mac—bless him, stayed with her until she fell asleep."

Rainy piped in, "Since we're not going to be there today, I'm sending my assistant to stay with her. Starting tomorrow, we've got a schedule all worked out so she won't be alone."

He made his way around the table and placed a kiss on the top of Rainy's head. "Well good morning, Mrs. Anderson. Don't you look beautiful this morning? How's married life with the Runt treating you?" Her expression softened as she quickly glanced at Terry. "Married life is wonderful. Thank you for asking."

Nathan couldn't hide his grimace when he saw his client. The man looked like death warmed over. "Thank you for helping out with Amy, Mac. The timing couldn't be worse. I appreciate you staying with her. I'm sure she's grateful."

Mac sipped his coffee and then responded, "It's no problem. With everything that's happening today on the ranch, there's no way I could've slept last night anyway."

Nathan leaned against a chair. "Okay. Now that Amy's squared away, at least for the time being, we can focus on Mac's problem.

"It's cold outside, so I set Bright Flower and Spirit Keeper up in the tent that you used for the wedding. I turned the patio heaters on so we wouldn't freeze our butts off out there," Nathan explained.

The longer he stood, the more his legs felt like rubber. Whatever was in that potion last night had kicked his ass. He decided to plunk himself down at the table before his legs gave out altogether. Not being a heavy drinker, his head pounded from the worst hangover he'd ever suffered. An expansive yawn escaped as he rubbed his grainy eyes. Jody placed her small hands on his shoulders. "You look a little under the weather. We need you today. Are you going to be up for this?"

Knowing his dear friend, Jody, was a mother hen, Nathan reached up and patted her hand to ease her mind. "It was a long night. We were up late at the camp, but when we finally went to bed, I slept like the dead. I'll be fine."

Being the perfect hostess, Jody started passing around plates and silverware to her guests. Nathan said, "Spirit Keeper and Bright Flower wanted to get started with the preparations right away. I need everyone's ammunition. They want to bless it before we leave."

Jared's eyebrow rose. "Don't get me wrong. I plan on going in loaded for bear. But I thought we were dealing with spirits? How in the world will bullets be effective?"

Nathan couldn't begin to explain what he'd witnessed last night. Even if he could, no one would believe him. They'd just have to see for themselves. "Their ways are different. Keep an open mind. I learned things last night that I wouldn't have thought possible yesterday morning. Spirit Keeper will fill everyone in on the details. For now, though, get the ammunition you're taking. Don't leave anything out. *Everything* must be blessed."

Jared eyed him for another few moments before rising. "Okay. Whatever you say. The ammo is locked up. I'll grab it for you."

Still a little loopy, Nathan could swear the bacon was calling to him. A biscuit was a much wiser choice, so he snatched one of those up instead. Tossing the soft, warm bread into his mouth, he hoped his irritated stomach would accept the peace offering. "We'll need about a half-hour before you join us, so eat fast."

The house rumbled as two low flying helicopters zoomed over the roof. Everyone inside watched through the big picture window as they landed in the far meadow behind the cabin. The mood in the room changed from subdued to anxious in the blink of an eye. Game time was fast approaching. Soon, they'd all load themselves into those choppers and fly off to their very own episode of a horror show.

Mac nudged Nathan. "I understand the helicopters are taking us in, but I don't understand how we're supposed to navigate through that disgusting mud. The muck is going to make our fight much harder."

Nathan replied, "I discussed this with Spirit Keeper this morning. He said that the land is like a sponge. It absorbs the water quickly. I don't know how that's possible, but he believes it will be dry when we get there."

Jared returned and Nathan grabbed the offered ammunition cans. He swiped one more biscuit, saluted everyone, and stepped through the back door to join his new family in their preparations.

Chapter Eighteen

Bright Flower had started a small fire and was fueling it when the rest of the group entered the wedding tent. Spirit Keeper appeared to be light years away in his own little world unaware of their arrival. The blaze cast deep shadows in the old man's facial crevices making him look more dead than alive.

Jody and Jared sat to Spirit Keeper's left. Terry and Rainy took their place across the fire. Mac knelt to their left, and Nathan and Bright Flower squatted to the old man's right. The circle was complete.

Bright Flower passed the ammunition storage containers back to Jared. "I have dusted all of the bullets with ash—a gift from the Creator. I wiped all of the ammunition off so no harm would come to any one of our group when they touch the bullets."

Jared offered a confused smile and replied, "Thank you."

Spirit Keeper raised his eyes and stared at all that sat around the fire before speaking. "I asked that we join here at this consecrated ground where Spirit Talker and her man married not six months ago, and where the witch and her man married yesterday. These unions are potent. We are all connected to the Earth and its vibrations. The Creator smiles upon the couplings and this sacred place, and so we shall use the power to bless our journey into the battle with darkness.

Spirit Keeper raised his arm above his head and slammed the antler he held onto the hide of the drum. The force behind the unexpected movement startled everyone in attendance and spurred the group to jump in unison. The old man's eyes rolled back deep into his head as he started to chant. The haunting sound captured everyone's full attention. One after the other, each person closed their eyes and allowed the cadence to bathe their bodies and fill their souls. The old man sang and trilled for fifteen minutes, anointing everyone with his special power of song.

After helping Spirit Keeper to his feet, Bright Flower passed him a bowl. The old man stood between the fire and Nathan as he dipped his finger into the dark liquid. Speaking in English so everyone in attendance could understand his intent, his hand shot up to the heavens. "Creator, I call upon you to bless this paint with your essence. With your fury, shield the wearer from the evil we face."

Spirit Keeper's finger slashed in a crooked line down both of Nathan's cheeks. The zig zag motion led him to believe crudely painted lightning bolts now covered his face. Grateful he wasn't standing, Nathan felt every muscle in his body contract as a surge of electricity shocked his system.

"The Navajo people are not known for wearing war paint, but we must protect ourselves with the sign of the Creator's wrath and vengeance. The inhabitants of the cursed land come from many different tribes. It does not matter from which clan the lost souls we will face today were born into. The evil spirits will recognize the mark, and it will give them pause. Depending on how far from humanity the individual cursed souls have traveled, this symbol should strike fear in our enemy and make the majority think twice about attacking." Each person around the fire received the smeared stain of the Creator on both cheeks. When done, Spirit Keeper stood in front of Nathan again.

Bright Flower handed her grandfather another vessel, this one filled with crushed, dried plants. He took a pinch between his fingers and drew a letter X over Nathan's heart while speaking in his native language. The gnarled hand opened, and the aged Singer blew the flakes onto his head before moving on to the next person. After everyone had been anointed in the same manner, the old man took his spot and sat. His advanced age was evident to all in the way he struggled for balance.

"We will arrive ten minutes before the total eclipse. Doing so will give us just enough time to draw the enemy out of hiding." Turning his attention to Jared, he said, "The timing is important." Jared glanced down at his watch and nodded. Nathan was fully aware that his partner never went into any altercation without being familiar with every aspect. That being the case, he was positive Jared already had this breach planned out down to the minute.

Spirit Keeper nodded his approval before continuing. "Once we have been dropped off, the helicopters must leave. They should be nearby though, in case escape is necessary. If we are not successful, no one will make it off of the land alive by foot."

Jared offered his assurance. "After we disembark, the pilots have instructions to land at a field just outside of St. Johns. They will wait for us to conclude our business. Nathan has told me the land is so remote that cell phones do not work. In case of emergency, I will provide everyone with a satellite phone. If needed for rescue, the choppers can be there to pick us up in fifteen minutes."

Spirit Keeper offered a pleased grin. "That is good to hear.

"My people are fearful of the eclipse so the lingering spirits will be cautious. Once we are on the ground, we will stand in a circle with our backs together while Bright Flower places peace offerings around us. Be aware. Most of you will not have the ability to see the enemy. They *are* there. We will be surrounded within a matter of minutes. Over the years I've learned that our enemy's regular pattern is to slither through the night and hide during the day. Once they recognize the threat we present, they will come forward and out into the open. Not even the eclipse will keep them at bay. *This* action will be their undoing.

"Spirit Talker, you are gifted with sight whereas we are blind. You must be vocal and tell us all that you see."

Everyone's attention zeroed in on Jody. "I will do this."

Spirit Keeper scanned the men. "Warriors, you have your weapons. Nathan is familiar with his and is aware of the potency. Your ammunition has been anointed with the Creator's ash. Once fired you may or may not see the results of the bullets, but the power unleashed when shot will frighten the spirits and even stop them if it comes to that. If their essence is touched by the Creator's wrath, which your bullets have been consecrated in, their soul will implode and disappear.

Their existence will be turned to dust and lost forever. Know this to be true, and you may survive.

"Due to the sheer number of evil spirits, they could believe they are immune to destruction. That being the case, the skinwalkers may appear as solid beings to incite fear in their enemy. This is the time when they are at their most vulnerable—*and* when they are at their most dangerous. I am warning you these creatures are an abomination—a combination of wild animal and man. Our enemy's form is hideous. Do not let this distract you. They thrive on the weaknesses of soul and character. I caution all of you that if they make themselves visible, do *not* look into the eyes of the enemy. They are powerful beings who can and will take your soul and occupy your bodies. Their way into your body is through your eyes.

"Show no fear. To do so means your death. If you become fearful, you *must* tamp it down immediately." Spirit Keeper tapped his head. "Remember a time in your life when fear overtook you. Once that emotion dissipated anger was left in its wake. Fear *always* begets anger. Allow the weakness of fear to turn into blinding rage—feel the wrath swirl and build in your gut until it can no longer be controlled. Clench your fists and let that fury escape in a fierce war cry. The vibration of that scream will stop the enemy short. They will be confused and need a moment to regain their purpose.

"These supernatural beings have *never* been confronted by living people before. Through dream quest, I have traveled often to this place but never in physical form. It was too dangerous. If any unsuspecting person wandered onto the land, the skinwalkers always had the upper hand. Their master has done them a great disservice. My brother has made them believe they are invincible. These spirits will not know how to react when *we* seek *them* out."

The men glanced at one another and solemnly nodded.

"Our goal is to rid the land of the damaged spirits. Only then can Bright Flower address the property's curse. We cannot open the gates to heal the land until the skinwalker threat has been dealt with one way or another.

"Witch, you have great power. The Creator has spoken and given permission to deviate from my people's rigid death rituals. There are too many spirits to make the journey across the Navajo Nation to the Underworld on foot. My people would be in jeopardy. Therefore, it will be your task to create a bridge from this desolate land to the Underworld. Even though these demented souls have not undergone the proper burial rituals, the spirits willing to accept His gifts will be allowed to cross and thrive in His presence. The Creator will accept those lost souls who wish to move on and reunite with their long-lost families. The bridge will be the only option for them to proceed to the Creator's side. All remaining spirits who fail to make the journey across the bridge must die the eternal death dealt by the warriors before you now. You will enter the center of the circle once Bright Flower has finished presenting the peace offerings. The others will shield you from the enemy while you summon the bridge."

Rainy clutched her athame with one hand and squeezed Terry's leg with the other. "I understand. It will be done just as you have requested."

"Once we clear the land, Bright Flower will remove the wards placed centuries ago that were meant to keep the evil ensnared within their boundaries." Spirit Keeper sought out Mac's attention. "My granddaughter must be granted access to the land monthly to make peace offerings. These continued gifts are the only way healing will be possible. The land has been touched by evil for so long that the earth will require attention for many years to mend what has been tainted."

Mac nodded his assent. Spirit Keeper fell quiet and stared into the blaze.

The rancher took this opportunity to voice his concerns. "Excuse me, sir. How will your brother be dealt with? It seems to me that the problem will only continue if he is allowed to stay."

Spirit Keeper nodded, but he offered no answer. Bright Flower spoke in his stead. "My grandfather is the only one that can stop his brother. The man and beast that lives within my great-uncle's body is a practitioner of The Witchery Way—my people's most evil magic. He is blood and flesh but no longer human—only wickedness at its purest. The Creator will not have him. Nothing will save the boy he used to be. He must perish at my grandfather's hand."

Bright Flower's voice hitched, and Nathan gently rubbed her back for strength. "There is only one way to kill a creature such as this one—a living, breathing skinwalker. My grandfather must be close enough to look into his eyes and speak his brother's birth name. Only this will weaken him enough to bring eternal death."

Rainy lurched forward. "What is Spirit Keeper's

plan for safety? If his brother is in animal form, your grandfather could be torn to shreds if he gets that close."

A single tear rolled down Bright Flower's cheek. Her lips quivered before regaining composure. "My grandfather believes he will not survive."

Everyone gasped and started talking all at once.

Nathan drowned the concerned voices out as the dreaded private conversation that he and Mac had with Spirit Keeper resurfaced—the exchange that had occupied the forefront of his mind ever since. The old man had sworn them to secrecy. But Nathan knew full well that when the time came to share, the secret could mark the end of his marriage. A cold chill riddled with anxiety forced an involuntary shiver. Nathan and Mac shared a glance with downturned lips.

"Enough," Spirit Keeper shouted. "I have tried for years to get close enough to kill my brother. Unlike the wandering spirits that follow him, his physical body must not die before I utter his name. He is cagey and so powerful that I fear nothing could stop him if he were allowed to shed his physical body before I utter his name.

"If his minions—the beasts—appear before you, shoot your weapons at them. The Creator's ash will destroy them. Do not—even if you have a clear shot— do *not* fire upon their master."

With a shaky hand, Spirit Keeper raised the antler and pointed at Nathan. "There will come a time when my brother is distracted. Use your bow. Maim him. Do whatever is necessary to immobilize him so that I may do what must be done to destroy him. Only after I speak his name can he be mortally wounded. Otherwise, his malevolence will live on and may never be equalized."

****

Time was short, and the helicopters moved swiftly across the darkening sky—while the moon slowly ate away at the sun's rays. Nathan held tight to his bride hoping that when the battle was over, she'd find forgiveness in her heart for his actions. Nathan and Mac had both given their word of honor that they would follow her grandfather's wishes to the tee even over Bright Flower's vehement objections. The old man's solemn words continued to repeat through Nathan's mind. *"My granddaughter will not understand. She will fight you. And when she can't win, she will spurn you. But you must follow through. In time I will give her a sign that all is as it should be. Until then, she will despise you for ordering her to abandon the Navajo Way of things. You must stay strong in the face of her anger. This is how it must be."*

"We're almost there." The harshness of Mac's voice snapped Nathan out of his mental deliberations. Over the last several days he'd become fond of the rancher who was ready and willing to battle even the unknown for what was his. His eyes were cold and squinted against the sun—reflecting a fierceness that matched the snarl on his lips. Nathan would never want this man as an enemy.

The pilot's voice snapped out, "There's the four-wheeler, Nathan. Jared gave us instructions to land here if the ground wasn't too muddy. It looks as though everything has dried out." The radio hissed alive. "Chopper One to Chopper Two. You got me?"

The pilot opened the radio mic. "Chopper Two has you Chopper One."

"Boss man says to do a flyover and recon the area. Chopper One will stay here above the landing area to make sure all remains clear of combatants."

"Affirmative, Chopper One. Chopper Two out." Nathan's helicopter flew just high enough over the treetops to scan the land for any evidence of movement. After finding nothing amiss, they returned to the prearranged landing spot.

"Chopper One, all clear from Chopper Two. Nothing visible on recon."

"Chopper One to Chopper Two, our landing spot looks copasetic." Nathan heard Jody's excited voice interrupt the pilot on Chopper One but couldn't make out all of what she was saying. After a moment of silence, the radio squawked back to life. "U-m-m...Chopper Two...Chopper One here. A-h-h...female passenger on Chopper One wants me to convey that she sees no...U-m-m...no ghosts."

Nathan burst out laughing. His pilot turned back to him with a quizzical expression. "Sir, how do you want me to respond to that?"

"Just copy."

"All righty then." The pilot pressed the mic and stated clearly, "Copy that, Chopper One. No ghosts. What are the boss man's orders?"

"Chopper One to Chopper Two, the previous muddy conditions have reversed. The boss man says it's show time. We're good to go. I'll land east. You land just west of me. Chopper One out."

Chapter Nineteen

They got lucky. The ground had indeed dried out enough they didn't have to deal with the unforgiving mud, but not enough for the super fine dust to choke them. Everyone quickly disembarked and formed a circle between the two helicopters. The engines powered up, and the rotors spun faster and faster lashing the group with a cold gale force wind. The anxiety of watching those choppers abandoning them in the middle of hell punched Nathan in the solar plexus. He took a deep breath to calm himself and glanced at his watch. *Ten minutes. We just have to survive for ten minutes.*

All but Nathan were armed to the teeth with fully automatic rifles. The guns were against the law, and under ordinary circumstances would never be used, but there was no threat of jail time here. They needed a fast and accurate way to spray the real weapon—the bullets which the Creator himself had supercharged. If the ammo proved to be half as effective as the bow, they should be able to handle the threat.

Nathan bowed his head and said a quick prayer as he tightened his fist around the bow. Fully aware of the danger lurking in every shadow, he plucked the first of many arrows from the quiver and loaded his ancient weapon.

They took up their positions back to back—each person having their own area to defend. Once the circle was complete Spirit Keeper announced their presence by pounding on his drum and trilling in his native language. Terry nudged Nathan's shoulder. "Why isn't the old man in the circle with us? What's he doing?"

Nathan looked into his best friend's eyes and saw the gut-twisting fear just beneath the surface. Terry, more of a brother than a friend, was not now nor had he ever been an Alpha. He was a jokester—a fun loving artist that currently found himself far out of his depth. History with this man had shown that no matter how difficult the task proved to be Terry could be counted on to lighten the mood. He'd always found a way to dig deep and display great bravery when facing the unknown and the terrifying. Given a choice, Nathan would choose his friend in battle over anyone else. Pride at being associated with a man such as this settled in Nathan's heart as he comforted Terry with an arm slung over his slight shoulders. "Get ready, Runt. Spirit Keeper is calling them out." Terry momentarily blanched losing all color in his face. Nathan gave him a few moments to recover his lost courage. His friend didn't disappoint. He stiffened under the weight of Nathan's arm and regained his composure. "I'm ready."

"Remember, Runt, show no fear."

Terry bit down hard on his lip and bobbed his head. "That reminds me of a joke. Have you heard the one—"

Jody raised her voice so everyone could hear, "I don't see anything yet." She continued to slowly turn and take in as much of the landscape as possible.

Terry's lips puckered as he raised his shoulders. "I guess I'll have to wait to tell you the punch line. It was a good one, too."

Bright Flower roamed just outside the circle and stopped in front of Nathan. She dropped the duffle bag and started rooting through the contents. Placing an intricately painted clay bowl at his feet, she filled the basin to the brim with bits of shredded wood and ground plants. A brilliant spark from a fire starter quickly ignited the dry mixture releasing more smoke than Nathan would've thought possible. Fanning the impressive cloud with a large feather, she moved in and out of the circle covering everyone from back to front and head to toe with the fragrant woodsy scent. Once all had been smudged Bright Flower stood her ground in front of Mac. She held the bowl up to the heavens offering the remains to whatever spirits hid just out of sight. His bride knelt in front of the rancher and scooped a hole in the earth with her free hand. The still burning embers were placed at his feet.

The feather imbued with smoke was positioned in front of Rainy.

Bright Flower drew a sack of apples from the duffle bag. Offering the ripe, aromatic fruit to the sky her voice trilled an ancient call. The primordial sound struck a chord deep in Nathan's soul and left goosebumps in its wake. Freeing a sharp dagger from a sheath at her calf, Bright Flower carefully cut and then placed half of an apple in front of everyone. When she reached Jody, the last apple was cut and presented to the spirits before being arranged at her feet.

Bright Flower repeated the same steps with an ear of corn. Once offered to the spirits, the cob was positioned in front of Jared.

Two arrowheads, one light and one dark, were

dropped into a bowl of water. Bright Flower paraded around the group spraying droplets of water from her fingertips on each member. The remaining contents of the bowl were poured at Terry's feet.

Bright Flower's final offering was a pipe made from clay. Nathan's only experience with such an object came from western movies, and they had always been carved from wood. This ceremonial pipe was vastly different from anything he'd ever seen before. The mouthpiece was formed into the image of a bird's head. He could imagine Bright Flower or even Spirit Keeper painstakingly pinching and prodding the clay into just the right shape. The cylinder had been painted white with black and brown geometric shapes to represent feathers. The pipe was a thing of beauty. The object looked far too fragile to be used for anything other than rituals. Bright Flower packed the bowl with loose tobacco. Once lit, she puffed and made a production of dropping tobacco flakes at everyone's feet. Grasping the object with both hands, she lifted the pipe to the sky as the final offering to the spirits. The smoldering pipe was then positioned at Nathan's feet.

"Still nothing," Jody hollered.

Nathan shifted his weight and glanced at his watch—only five minutes had passed. It seemed like a lifetime. *Why haven't they shown themselves?* He prayed he hadn't led his friends into a blood bath. The odds of everything going off without a hitch were incalculable. They were only eight to defend this land. The enemy numbered in the hundreds, maybe even thousands. If this motley group were to fail, they would all die a gruesome death—mangled and torn to pieces. *What have I done?*

Vengeful Spirits

If any one of them were to die at the hands of these creatures, what would happen to their souls? Would they be tortured throughout eternity, damned to live as some kind of half-human half-animal abomination? Or would they simply rise to Heaven never the wiser?

Time seemed to drag on forever. As the seconds ticked off, more and more questions filled Nathan's mind. He would swear that he felt his sanity slipping. Panic started to set in and eat away at his confidence. *What if I can't protect the people I love?* That thought jarred him. His heartbeat sped up even faster and breathing became difficult. He licked suddenly dry lips to moisten them, but all his saliva had long since dried up. Unable to swallow, Nathan reached up and grasped his throat hoping to coax a clear breath for his oxygen-starved lungs. Pinpricks of light floated in and out of his field of vision. Everything was slowly vanishing and going black. His knees started to buckle under the strain when a loud snort sounded in his ear. His buffalo grunted its displeasure and hooked Nathan's arm with a massive horn to keep him upright. Nathan locked his gaze onto the beast's dark eyes and drew strength from the animal's fighting spirit. Slowly he regained his calm. Bright Flower grasped his hand and offered a gentle caress for reassurance.

Jody shouted, "Black shadows! I can't make out any features yet. They are just inky blobs moving through the tree line." She audibly gasped, and her voice quivered, "Oh my God! There are hundreds of them. They're holding their ground and not making a move—yet." Everyone raised their weapons.

Rainy, ready to conjure the bridge, moved to the center of the circle and yanked a ceremonial athame from her waistband.

"They're jutting in and out the trees now! They seem to be getting bolder with their movements." Stress and fear laced Jody's voice, raising it an octave higher.

Nathan's buffalo lowered its head and chuffed. Ropes of saliva poured from the beast's mouth as it kicked at the dirt readying itself for battle. Its massive head swung from side to side daring the enemy to come near.

The shriek of a raptor sounded above them. Bright Flower's eagle soared over their heads protecting the high ground.

A deep throaty yowl sounded to Nathan's right. Standing tall, twenty-five feet from the circle, Spirit Keeper reached out and lovingly patted the mountain lion's head. He shooed the animal with his hand to leave his side and join the group. The puma stood in place refusing to move a step. Spirit Keeper bent and rubbed his cheek between the animal's ears. He stared into the golden eyes of his spirit animal and then roughly pushed him away, rebuking him so he would leave the old man to go fight next to the others. The cat unleashed an agonizing roar and reluctantly took its place next to the circle. Glancing around, it became apparent to Nathan, he and his bride were the only people in the circle able to see the unusual animal alliance that had joined their group in battle. Jody was too preoccupied watching the enemy to be aware of their presence.

Spirit Keeper threw his shoulders back and bellowed to the spirits in the trees. The old man's voice belied his age, conveying power and authority as he shouted in his native tongue to the creepy crawlies surrounding them.

Jody's arm flew into the air and frantically pointed heavenward as an unbridled scream broke free sending a jolt of unadulterated fear throughout the group. "What is that?"

Everyone turned in unison and got their first glimpse of the horror they'd be facing. A massive winged animal flew low over the trees. Each flap of the wings whipped at the dense copse of pine trees, bending their tops almost to the breaking point.

The creature moved with ease through the air. Horrified by the vision of a half man, half animal in mid-flight Nathan was stymied by the fact that an abomination such as this could soar with the grace and speed of a large predatory owl.

Huge talon-edged feet jutted out and reached for the ground. The man-beast landed between their protected circle and the malevolent shadows hiding in the trees. The hideous monster stood eight-feet-tall. This creature was a witch doctor on steroids. *Is this real or just an illusion manifested by a dark arts practitioner?* Massive black wings stretched out in a twenty-foot span. A terrifying headdress covered in feathers and horns pivoted from side to side as the entity gazed at the people within the circle. The abomination's eyes beneath the mask glowed a deep molten red. Wolf pelts covered the creature's shoulders with the fur extending down to its navel. The man-beast arched his deformed body and threw its head back— unleashing an unearthly, wicked shriek. Nathan recognized that cry from the night they were stuck in the line shack. The chilling sound was not avian, mammal, nor was it human. Rather an obscene cross between the three.

Jody yelled, "The black shadows are working themselves up into a frenzy. They're moving so fast that I can no longer tell them apart as separate beings. All I can see is one large swirling haze."

Rainy's voice seeped into Nathan's consciousness. There wasn't a single hint of a flutter in her tone. She was putting on a strong front as she called out her intentions loud and clear. "Mother Goddess, hear my words. The spirits on this land are unclean. The Creator has offered forgiveness and a safe haven for all of those willing to shed the evil that ties them to this land. Their deity offers asylum in the Underworld. It is our task to provide the means for travel."

Nathan clenched his teeth. *Hurry, hurry, hurry.*

Rainy's chant infuriated the skinwalker master. The Navajo dark lord focused his anger on her. A low, menacing growl echoed through the air. "I will kill you, witch. Your magic is not as strong as mine. Unless you stop your spell, I will tear you from limb to limb. You are on *my* land. I demand that you stop and bow to me." The guttural demonic tone of the skinwalker's voice covered Nathan in goosebumps.

Terry moved to the center of the circle to protect his wife. Rainy, God love her, never missed a beat. "I beseech you, Mother Goddess, to provide a bridge of light and love from this soiled land to the blessed Underworld. Let the love of Heaven and Earth shine brightly as these beings are called home. I ask for this act of love and forgiveness in the Creator's name." Her athame rose skyward, and a glimmer of golden light ripped through the eclipse-shadowed horizon. As the fissure opened, lightning coursed through the sky.

"So mote it be."

Angry war cries came out of nowhere and mixed with coyotes yipping in excitement. Jody, horrified by what she saw, covered her ears as she violently shook her head in disbelief. "Oh my God! The shadows are changing. They're pulsing and becoming more solid.

"They're coming out!" She had a difficult time catching her breath. Jared grabbed her arm and shook her. "Remember, don't look into their eyes."

Deep rumbling thunder rolled through the air. The rift in the sky that Rainy's spell had created grew larger and brighter in direct contrast with the darkness of the solar eclipse.

Nathan shielded his eyes as he chanced a glance at the now rapidly opening fissure. "Hurry, hurry, hurry," he whispered.

Brilliant drops of light started to cascade down from the rift as if fluid rain.

Spirit Keeper remained calm and continued to speak to those spirits willing to listen.

Tensions were quickly escalating. Nathan snapped at Bright Flower, "What is Grandfather saying to them?"

"He's explaining that all but their leader can be saved. The bridge of light which is forming will lead them into the arms of their ancestors. If they so choose, the ties that bind them to the evil one will break, and they will be set free. Before crossing, they must drop the pelts that act as their bondage and rebuke their master and all of his teachings."

The sheer pressure of this situation was affecting Jody. Her voice cracked, and she had to clear her throat before being able to relay how the enemy was behaving. "They're not acting aggressively. They seem to be listening to what Spirit Keeper is telling them." She gasped and took a slight step back. "They're slowly moving toward us." Jody bent at the waist and clutched her knees. "They're hideous. I've never dreamed there could be such evil in this world."

Mac cried out, "I can see Spirit Keeper's brother— or the beast he's become. Beyond him I see glowing yellow-green orbs circling and swirling through the air. Are those the spirit skinwalkers?"

"Yes," Jody screamed. "Their eyes are shining a weird iridescent yellowish color."

The rancher spun in a quick circle. "My God! They're all around us!"

The dark master took flight. He was on Rainy in half a second. The creature swooped in and swiped at her back with a large talon. Its claws tangled in her sweater and for a brief, terrifying moment lifted her off the ground. Bright Flower's eagle dived and hit the skinwalker's headdress. The frightening mask slipped but didn't fall. Terry landed a solid blow with the butt of his rifle. Rainy swung her arm high, and the athame sliced through the air hitting its mark—slashing the creature's muscular leg. The skinwalker's blood splashed across Terry's face. The beast screeched in anger and released his hold on Rainy.

"Attack!" The coward took to the sky as an army of iridescent orbs advanced on the group.

The Creator's ash-covered bullets did their job as yellow-green orbs blinked out of existence when the group blasted the automatic rifles in all directions. "Hold your fire," Jody yelled. "They're retreating."

Spirit Keeper stood all alone twenty-five feet from

the circle. An easy target, his brother was on the old man in an instant. The creature's talons dug into the soft tissue on Spirit Keeper's shoulders and lifted him off of the ground. Blood spewed from the wounds. They were in mid-flight as Nathan raised the bow. Knowing he couldn't deal a fatal blow, he called on a higher power, "Creator, this arrow is an extension of your supremacy. Let your will be done and allow your wrath to fly true." A clap of thunder bellowed as the projectile flew. The arrow ignited in flight and flames parted the sky. The creature's wing combusted in fire and then exploded. The Navajo dark lord screamed and dropped Spirit Keeper. The old man's body slammed to the earth in a broken heap. Unable to maintain flight the beast followed his brother out of the sky, tumbling through the air and landing on top of Spirit Keeper.

Somehow the old man found the strength to roll while wildly brandishing a knife. He struck his brother in the well-muscled thigh but was careful not to wield a death blow.

The evil one scratched and clawed with its talons trying to find a way to expose the old man's neck. Its massive head lowered and found its mark. Blood spurted from Spirit Keeper's throat as flesh was torn and ripped. With his final living breath, the old man rolled his head and whispered into the evil one's ear.

Spirit Keeper's brother recoiled and shrieked as if the spoken words maimed him. Rising up with his deformed and taloned feet, the weakened creature stumbled and fell. The beast crawled back to its prey and ripped into Spirit Keeper's body.

Nathan's belly swelled with rage. He allowed the fury to move through his chest and up his throat. The emotional war cry he released was full of pain and regret and sent shockwaves through the air. His arrow whizzed from the bow and connected with the skinwalker's chest. The evil one burst into flames and then exploded leaving nothing of its existence behind.

Eerie high-pitched squeals sounded all around them. The threat wasn't over yet. Jody yelled, "The spirits seem to be fading in and out. They're confused." Excited yips echoed back to the group.

Liquid golden light poured from the fissure—a waterfall in the sky. "Bright Flower, the bridge is up. Call to them!"

The spirits' yips turned to fearful howls. Yellow-green eyes flashed while the ghosts scurried in and out of the trees.

Nathan screamed at Bright Flower, "The evil one is dead. Tell them they can leave this place." She stepped from the circle and knelt beside Spirit Keeper's body. She righted his drum and struck it with her fist. A mournful song filled the air, and the fluorescent eyes paused but made no move toward their only escape.

Voices from the sky joined Bright Flower in song, each heavenly note reverberating throughout Nathan's body. His attention turned to the light bridge. A woman, the one who'd approached him at Spirit Keeper's fire the night before, dared to leave the safety of the bridge. She walked straight into the den of the enemy and wrapped her arms around a single entity. The mist she held materialized as a misshapen solid human animal. The woman cupped the hideous face and kissed him. Nathan was too far away to hear what she said, but her intention was clear. She was bringing a loved one home. The skinwalker ripped the pelt from his back, and they ran for the bridge, then disappeared into the light.

Other ethereal beings crossed over and followed suit. Groups of people passed their circle and found their loved ones. Time seemed to stand still as the magical events played themselves out.

Jody searched the horizon. "I don't see any more skinwalkers."

Overcome with emotion the group fell to their knees. The flowing waterfall of light slowly subsided as the first rays of the mid-day sun broke through the moon's armor.

Chapter Twenty

Nathan approached Bright Flower as she knelt next to Spirit Keeper's mutilated remains. There were no tears. Shell shocked, she looked off into the distance past her grandfather's body as Nathan removed his coat and covered as much of the carnage as he could. The other men silently followed suit. Her stony expression never wavered. The pain his wife hid behind her blank features broke his heart.

The helicopters had to be called to bring the needed supplies. Nathan glanced at the people surrounding them and nodded to Jared. His friend pulled a satellite phone from his waistband and backed away from the group.

Nathan tugged Bright Flower into an embrace, but it took a few moments for her body to relax into his. On a sigh, she reached up and stroked his cheek. "We must hurry, Nathan. Grandfather must be returned home so I can properly bury him. I hope we're not too late for him to safely make his journey to the Underworld."

Nathan was aware of Mac standing behind them as he tightened his hold on Bright Flower. He knew the rancher was there to give moral support to follow through with the promise they'd both made to Spirit Keeper. "I'm so sorry, sweetheart, but we cannot move Grandfather. We must bury him here where he died.

There will be no death ritual. It was his wish."

Bright Flower's brow creased, and her breath faltered. Once the full impact of his words hit home, she shook her head violently. She pushed out of his embrace and defiantly stood with crossed arms. Time seemed to stand still as they stared at each other. Her hardened features slowly softened. "Nathan, you do not understand our ways. We must perform a death ritual and then the burial must take place on our property. It is the Navajo Way of things. The death ritual is the only means for grandfather to make the journey to the Underworld safely." As if no other explanation was necessary, she said, "Please hurry. We must work fast." He recognized her tone of voice. She was speaking to him as a teacher might to a student.

Bright Flower tugged on his shirt. Nathan bent down, and she caressed his cheek. The hard creases around her eyes disappeared and softened. If he could only make her understand that none of this was his idea. Spirit Keeper chose to defy the Navajo Way and remain here to watch over the land he'd given his life to save. His only role in this whole fucked up situation was to carry out a promise to a dying man. It was evident that she believed this situation was just a misunderstanding—nothing but another lesson for Nathan to learn in the Navajo culture. He felt sure that she believed once she'd made him aware of her people's traditions, he'd surely acquiesce. But that wasn't the case. The time had come to rip her heart out.

"I'm sorry. We cannot move him. Spirit Keeper will be buried here where he fell."

Bright Flower took a giant step back and teetered, almost falling to the ground. Nathan reached out to help her regain her balance, but she slapped his hand away. "No! I will not allow it. We must take him home now! It is imperative the burial ritual be performed. It is the Navajo Way." She thumped her chest with her fist. "It is *my* way."

Nathan stood alongside his wife and dreaded what he was about to say. *Please forgive me.* Needing to feel their connection he grabbed her shoulders and squeezed gently. "I'm sorry, sweetheart, but no. I cannot allow that to happen. Spirit Keeper left explicit directions on how he wanted to be buried. There will be *no* ritual. We will dig his grave right here."

Bright Flower struggled to free herself from his grasp. She slapped at his chest, and he let her go. "No! *You* are not Navajo. *You* do not understand. To do as you suggest would be cursing my grandfather. I will not have that! Spirit Keeper will be lost to walk the land for eternity without the ritual. *I will not allow it.*" Paralyzing venom filled each word. "Call the helicopters *now*. We must take him home."

Nathan's heart was pounding out of his chest. "No."

Looking to the others for support, Bright Flower's gaze wildly darted to the rest of the group and then landed on Mac. "My grandfather died today to help you. Out of respect, I insist that you follow my people's traditions."

Remorse and regret shaded Mac's eyes. "I'm sorry. But…"

She frantically turned away from the rancher and ran to Jared. "Please! Please! Call your helicopters so that I may bury my grandfather properly." Bright Flower collapsed into Jared's arms. The first tears started to fall. Pleading through her wails, she fisted her hand and struck his chest. "This must not happen. You can't condemn him to walk the earth throughout eternity. We must get him home immediately."

Nathan closed in and tried to pull her away from Jared, but she broke free and hit him in his solar plexus. Her eyes were wild and beyond reason. He had to make her understand. "Spirit Keeper—"

"Do not speak his name. *You* are not worthy," she hissed. Bright Flower made eye contact with everyone in the group. It was one last ditch effort for understanding and help. When her plea went unheeded, she screamed, "You have all betrayed my grandfather and me." His wife spun and ran toward the ridge.

Nathan started after her, but Mac stopped him. Tossing a rifle over his shoulder, he said, "I'll go after her and keep her safe." Rainy and Jody chimed in, "We'll go too." Mac clasped Nathan's arm. "It is your final duty to Spirit Keeper to carry out his wishes and do what must be done here. I owe a huge debt to that man. You must put your emotions to the side and follow his wishes. It is what he wanted. In time, she'll see it is the truth."

Mac pointed in the distance. "She's headed for the line shack. We'll take her there and make sure she's okay." He swallowed deeply. "Can you handle this?" The rancher tilted his head toward the body.

Nathan grimaced as he followed his wife's movements into the trees. He managed a nod but couldn't bring himself to speak. The thump-thump of the helicopters' blades signaled their return. Once the big choppers landed, the men off-loaded the equipment they needed.

As they worked silently to follow Spirit Keeper's explicit instructions, Nathan cursed the old man for putting him in this position with Bright Flower. There was no ritual. No words of sympathy were spoken. No tears. The ceremonial bow and arrow placed on his body before the earth covered him. That was the end of it. Nathan had followed every one of Spirit Keeper's last wishes. His duty to the man had been fulfilled. The time had come to face the consequences.

The men started to walk away when Nathan turned one last time to plead his case. "Send a sign, old man. The sooner, the better."

****

Nathan hesitated before knocking on the cabin door. Smoke billowed from the chimney, so he knew someone was inside. He tilted his head and tried to hear voices, but all was dead silent. *Not a good sign.* Jared's hand landed sharply on his shoulder and squeezed. "It'll be all right. She'll come around."

Nathan bowed his head and shrugged. "I hope so." But the look of utter disgust Bright Flower had shot him before she ran off had him wondering if she'd ever speak to him again.

Terry elbowed Nathan in the ribs and rubbed his stomach. "Today was a busy day. We've slain spirits. We've kicked the bird slash wolfman's ass. *And* if that weren't enough, we are badass curse destroyers. I'm gettin' kinda hungry. How much longer are you gonna make us wait until you grow the balls to knock on the door?"

Jared chuckled and covered his mouth.

"Fine," Nathan murmured. He lifted his fisted hand again but couldn't seem to gather the nerve to knock.

Finally, Terry shoved him aside and just walked in unannounced.

Bright Flower knelt on a sleeping bag in the middle of the room and stared at the fire. Her shoulders slumped forward in defeat.

Jody hugged Nathan and whispered in his ear, "She's been like this since we got here. Bright Flower won't speak or even look at us. I'm sorry, Nathan. We've tried to talk to her, but nothing we say is having any effect. I know you, so I understand your actions with Spirit Keeper's body were done in good faith. But I'm afraid that Bright Flower believes we've all betrayed her. I don't know how to make this right. She appears to be off in her own little world."

Rainy stepped over and handed Nathan a glass of water. "Why don't you see if you can get her to drink?" He accepted the glass but didn't move. He *had* betrayed her and her people. There was nothing he could say that would make this mess go away. Rainy patted his arm. "Go on. Talk to her. If she doesn't respond, just keep talking. If that doesn't work, then just sit with her."

****

While everyone had tried to give Nathan and Bright Flower space, it was a small cabin. He was fully aware that every spoken plea was heard. It had been the longest two hours of his life. Nathan had cajoled until he was blue in the face, and Bright Flower hadn't so much as twitched. She had shut everything and everyone out. Especially him. His heart sank. *She hates me.*

Jared knelt beside him. "It's getting late. The helicopters are waiting for us. We should probably get going."

Nathan glanced at Bright Flower and knew he'd have to haul her out kicking and screaming. Mac approached and answered for him. "I think the three of us will stay here tonight. We can make sure all's quiet on the land. We've got everything we need.

"In the morning we'll hike down to the four-wheeler and see if we can get it to start. If so, we'll go back to the ranch house and drive back to Flagstaff. If all else fails, we'll give you a call on the satellite phone, and you can come back and pick us up."

****

The night was quiet. Nathan fed the fire every couple of hours and then took his place beside his wife. He'd long since given up speaking. She continued to stare into the flames as if they held the answers to all of her questions. Never before had he seen someone so still. Ever vigilant he kept his place by her side. No way was he going to allow her to give up on him.

****

Nathan had just spent the longest, most miserable night of his life next to a woman who hated him so much, she refused to acknowledge him. Mac stirred in the corner of the cabin signaling that morning had finally arrived. Groaning he untangled himself from the sleeping bag and lifted his tall body off the floor. Nathan jumped when the man's hand landed squarely on his shoulder. When their eyes met, he found compassion. "I'll make some coffee."

Without saying a word, Bright Flower rose. Nathan was on his feet and by her side immediately. She crossed the room and laid a hand on the doorknob. "Where are you going?" Nathan tried to keep the hysterics out of his voice but failed.

Without looking at him, she responded, "I'm going home. Please do not follow me." Again, she tried to open the door, but Nathan stopped her. "We're out in the middle of nowhere. You can't walk from here. The closest town is fifty miles as the crow flies. You'll never make it, it's too far." Anguished, he rubbed his watering eyes. "Don't leave me."

Bright Flower opened the door and looked at him for the first time. "I am Navajo. I *will* make it." She scowled and turned her nose up at him.

Nathan couldn't take any more. He dropped his head in defeat. His wife took the first step out the door and then another out of his life. He heard a sharp intake of breath as it caught in her throat. His head jerked up in time to see her hand fly to her mouth.

Bright Flower looked as though she'd fall. "What's wrong?" He grabbed her elbow to keep her from tumbling over. She dropped to her knees and fingered a freshly picked orange flower. Snatching the posy from the wooden floor his sweet wife clutched it to her chest. Tears filled her eyes as she looked up to Nathan. "It's an Indian Paintbrush—my namesake. It's a gift from Grandfather."

Mac came up behind them and stood in the doorway. "Look, there!" He pointed to a spot just off of the porch. Another flower clipping had been picked and placed in plain view. Bright Flower crawled on her hands and knees across the wood planks and reached out for the orange bloom.

Nathan's chest tightened. This was significant. He knew it down to his bones. There hadn't been a single bloom in sight yesterday. "Grandfather left these," she wept and pointed to footprints left behind in the soft dirt. "It's a man and a cat. It's him. Nathan, it's Grandfather!" Bright Flower jumped to her feet and found another bloom just yards from the last one. "He's left a trail for us to follow. Hurry! Hurry!"

They were led back to the gnarled oak on the edge of the rise. Nathan almost fainted when he looked down on yesterday's battlefield. There was a sea of bright orange wildflowers gently blowing in the morning breeze.

A deep guttural yowl caught everyone's attention. A young man—a warrior—stood tall with a mountain lion by his side. Wearing nothing but buckskin pants and a red-velvet handkerchief tied around his forehead, the Indian raised a hand and held it out to them. A faint voice carried on the breeze. "Granddaughter, do not shame me in front of your man. I warned him of your venom, and there's no doubt he's felt the sting of your bite. Forgive him. He did as he was told."

Tears continued to fall down Bright Flower's cheeks as she peered up at Nathan. "He's young again. Age no longer cripples him. I'm sorry, Nathan. I should have trusted you. Can you forgive me?"

Nathan pulled his wife into a loving embrace and nearly passed out with relief.

Spirit Keeper, now forever young, threw his head back and trilled in victory while slowly fading from view. Her grandfather raised his hand one last time and waved his final goodbye. "Yá'át'ééh, my children."

Bright Flower tugged at Nathan's shirt and lifted her arms. He picked her up so he could kiss her nose. She flung her arms around his neck and wrapped her legs around his waist.

His wife laid her head on his shoulder and

whispered in his ear, "I love you."

Never wanting to let go, Nathan squeezed his new bride until she squeaked. Still clutching Bright Flower, he dropped to his knees and whispered, "Ayoó' aniíníshní."

It seemed his use of the Navajo language with such a simple phrase had surprised Bright Flower. She raised her head and captured Nathan's gaze with hers. "How did you know?"

"When Spirit Keeper told me of his plans and how angry you would be, he taught me how to say I love you in Navajo. He said it might come in handy."

A small smile crossed her lips as her finger covered his mouth. "Is that so?" She kissed his nose. "It worked. I have news from your family as well. Your mother had a long discussion with me at the wedding. She wants us to have children right away." The corners of his mouth rose beneath her finger.

She bit her lip to keep from laughing. "I too would like a child right away, but I refuse to name our baby Great Peanut. *You, not me* will have to explain this to her."

Recalling his sister's words, which seemed an eternity ago, Nathan looked down at Bright Flower before saying, "I personally like that name." Amidst the look of horror on his wife's face he burst into laughter.

A word about the author...

I've been an avid reader for years. To my husband's dismay, I have bookshelves full of books, rooms full of books, boxes full of books. My cars have books in them. I just can't seem to get rid of them after I read them. You don't know when you will want to read it again, right? My husband bought me a Kindle, which cut down on storage needs, but it opened me up to books I might never have experienced otherwise.

The biggest transition in my relationship with books occurred, however, when I, much to my surprise, became an author. I had started having dreams about people I didn't know. I started looking forward to my dreams every night. Then I realized that I was daydreaming about these people as well. I'd just be sitting there, and these people and their antics would pop into my mind. Finally, I gave in and began writing their story down, something I had never dreamed of.

My books invariably feature strong women. My husband, Michael, and I have raised two strong daughters, Pilar and Shandelle, and they inspire the characters in my stories. I've had fun with all the books I've written. I think the fact that I insert real events into my books, things that have actually happened in my family's lives, is like having a private joke.

Although I write romance novels, they always contain a paranormal twist. I imagine my future writings will always contain romance with strong women and men of character, influenced by events that reach beyond what we consider normal, and perhaps seasoned with a little touch of whimsy.

http://sandywolters.weebly.com/

www.ingramcontent.com/pod-product-compliance
Lightning Source LLC
Chambersburg PA
CBHW070450260626
47161CB00004B/1261